A

Anthony Masters's fi‎.......... .... stories for adults called *A P‎................................en he was only twenty-four. Since then he has establis.:ed a reputation as a popular and gifted author, writing both fiction and non-fiction for children and adults.

Anthony was particularly well known for exploring issues in the lives of young adults. His books about young men stranded between childhood and maturity – struggling with issues of trust and faced with difficult, sometimes violent, situations – convey very real and contemporary dilemmas brilliantly.

Anthony's presence in the world of children's books will be keenly missed. *Web of Terror,* his last book for young adults, was completed just before his untimely death in April 2003 and is a gripping example of Anthony's writing at its most thrilling.

Among Anthony's other books for the Orchard list are the slightly younger and action-packed *Predator* titles, and the acclaimed Black Apple novels for young adults *The Drop*; *Day of the Dead*, which was shortlisted for the Angus Award, and *Wicked*, chosen as one of the 100 Best Books by the Book Trust.

ANTHONY MASTERS
WEB OF TERROR

ORCHARD BOOKS

For Peter and Gillian Chubb

ORCHARD BOOKS
96 Leonard Street, London EC2A 4XD
Orchard Books Australia
32/45-51 Huntley Street, Alexandria, NSW 2015
ISBN 1 84121 832 4
A paperback original
First published in Great Britain in 2003
Text © Anthony Masters 2003
The right of Anthony Masters to be identified
as the author of this work has been asserted by him
in accordance with the Copyright, Designs and Patents Act, 1988.
A CIP catalogue record for this book is available from the British Library.
1 3 5 7 9 10 8 6 4 2
Printed in Great Britain
www.wattspub.co.uk

ONE

Patrick tripped over a root and fell into a sea of nettles, cursing. He lay still, listening to their clumsy pursuit, for the gang were falling about too – not over roots, but their own feet, or that was how it sounded.

The stinging heat rash of the nettles on his hands and face smarted badly, but Patrick knew that if he got up again they might hear him. They weren't *all* stupid. Cal was out there and no doubt he was enjoying the chase for the sport, as well as the thought of the hard beating Patrick would get when he was captured.

As he lay there, Patrick remembered the knocking on the door. The single knock, repeated over and over again, while his mother sat in her wheelchair, devising a plan of campaign at considerable risk to herself.

Patrick pressed his face hard down in the nettle bed, almost enjoying the stinging which helped to blot out the certainty that Cal would soon find him because he had nowhere to go, nowhere to hide.

The August night was warm. Crane flies had been fluttering in the house, blundering about in his brother Declan's room, attracted by the light streaming through the open window. Declan would lie in bed with the leggy creatures brushing his face like rippling silk.

Patrick had a horror of the things, but Declan seemed to love the demented fluttering of the crane flies. He had once shown Patrick their larvae – dark greyish-brown grubs known as leather jackets. They hatched under the soil and provided a treat for starlings, which would neatly peck them out of their earthly sanctuary.

'It's a miracle,' Declan had told Patrick. 'The grubs change from leather jackets into crane flies. It almost makes me believe in God!'

Patrick had shaken his head. 'I hate the things. They get trapped in webs and the spiders rip them apart while they're still wriggling.'

'Spiders aren't allowed in here.' Declan had been indignant. 'I don't let them spin a single strand of web in this room. It's a safe haven.'

'You'll be telling me the crane flies have their own language next.'

'And why not?' One of the leggy insects had perched on Declan's hand. 'The secret language of crane flies. Now that would be something.'

Patrick stiffened. The hullabaloo of the chase was nearer now. Should he get up and run, or should he stay here, half-buried in the nettles? The smarting sensation was beginning to recede, but his panic, which had temporarily subsided into a dull numbness, was ready to start up all over again. Straining his ears, he could hear Cal coming closer, bellowing his name, closing in.

Patrick had seen what their beatings could do when Kevin Drummond fell foul of them. He'd had his nose broken as well as his jaw and both arms. Wasn't one enough, for Christ's sake? That wasn't a beating. That was a massacre. Cal's own special brand.

Callum O'Farrell was short but powerfully built with broad shoulders and thick black hair cut close to his head. His father and grandfather before him looked much the same in their photographs, and both had been active members of the Cause, eventually imprisoned by the British. Even now, Cal's father, Liam O'Farrell, was inside. Cal was going the same way and Patrick both admired and feared him. He had the Cause and would do anything for the Cause. Anything. By contrast, Patrick felt inadequate. He had never wanted the Cause, but couldn't find anything else to believe in.

Suddenly, he could see their steel-capped boots in the torchlight and the shock waves broke through as he waited for them to find him. But the next minute they'd gone, crashing through the undergrowth, still yelling his name, swearing in the darkness, the pack hungry for blood, adrenalin surging.

Face down, Patrick smelt the earth. There was wild garlic somewhere, pungent, rank, and tickling his nose were the inescapable nettles. Couldn't you make nettle soup? Nettle tea? How bad would it taste?

Patrick tried to distract himself, burrowing further into the nettle bed, absorbing more stings. He'd rather accept the earth's punishment than Cal's.

He thought of his old friend and now recent enemy again, seeing his tattooed arms, legs with muscles like steel and enough hatred in his heart to maim and kill. He'd seen him in action at school often enough; Cal winning playground fights that the teachers sought to stop, but were never able to break up fast enough to avoid injury.

What the hell was he going to do? Where could he find shelter? Patrick knew he couldn't hide here much longer, for Cal was never less than thorough and would get the gang to retrace their steps.

Slowly, still smarting, Patrick got to his feet. Were they hiding? Still waiting to pounce? That was all too possible for he could hear no sounds of the chase now.

The deep woods were silent, as if all small animals were hiding too, but ready to give Patrick away, even the voles, the stoats, the weasels and the foxes. Cal had put a spell on the Wildwood. It was bewitched.

The childish fantasy made Patrick feel a sudden

shame. He was fifteen. What was the matter with him?

He thought of his mother in her wheelchair in the kitchen, and Declan in his room, giving the crane flies a break, providing them with sanctuary. That was what Patrick needed right now – sanctuary. But where to get it? He knew these woods were close to the border, but even if he got over he'd have to come back. He imagined the gang swaggering down the street, heading for his door, confident they'd get him this time. The knock. The single knock. Later repeated again and again.

Thanks to Mum, he had gone through the toilet window, pulling himself out, dropping on to the ground and beginning to vault the fences before he was seen.

But suppose they hurt his mother in their anger? Suppose they went upstairs and had a go at Declan? Suppose they killed them both? Patrick gave an involuntary, half-strangled sob.

He knew they'd hurt him badly if he was caught. The thought of the pain made him want to throw up. Did his mother know the extent of it? Did she know what they were going to do? She had seemed calm – too calm – as she had planned his escape and how she would hold them off at the door, her wheelchair blocking the way until they were forced to push her aside, maybe even overturn the chair.

Cal was a childhood friend. They had played football together, gone to school together. Yet Cal would be the first to start the beating.

Then, in his desperation, Patrick suddenly remembered the house on the far side of the woods. An old man – an old soldier – lived there. He'd come to open the school fête. The Head had been excited at the thought of prising the old man from his retreat, out of his retirement. The Head had also made sure the boys knew the Colonel had nothing to do with the British army that still occupied their streets and raided their houses; he had belonged to another kind of British army, which had fought battles in faraway countries. 'He's a war hero,' the Head had told his students at assembly. 'A man who was decorated for serving his country.' Colonel Ernest Springfield, veteran of the Second World War, had fought in France, been captured and taken to a prisoner-of-war camp in Germany. A man with a record. A record of bravery.

In the flesh, Colonel Springfield had been a little disappointing – a tall, thin, stick of a man with sagging jowls and brown age-spots all over his face and hands, a beak-like nose and a hesitant way of speaking, as if he'd spent so much time alone, holed up in his now rotting old house, that he'd forgotten how to say words, let alone make them understood.

The Colonel had read from a script held in a

trembling hand and it hadn't been much of a speech at that, just a few stumbling sentences about the school fête. He'd gone away in a taxi, maybe unwilling to suffer any more, needing to get back behind the high walls of the house to which he had retreated so many years ago.

'He's a sad old sod,' Cal had said. 'We should go out there and see if he's got anything worth having.' But there was something about Colonel Springfield that had stopped them doing that.

Declan had said, 'He looks like a crane fly; those thin legs and arms, they're so wispy they could stick to you and break off.'

Patrick had shuddered. Why was Declan so strange? He'd been strange ever since Dad left for England, to be 'useful to the Cause' and, eventually, to take part in a pub bombing. Dad had been caught and was now in jail in the north of England, sentenced to life imprisonment, except that his mother had said with a false cheerfulness that 'he'll be home soon. They'll let him out. Someone will let him out.'

The yelling and the crashing of the hunters suddenly broke out again on the other side of the wood, but the mossy, overgrown wall of the Colonel's house was now only metres away.

Columbine House. Patrick had at last remembered the name – that stupid-sounding name which wasn't fit for a Colonel. Surely the house should be named after a famous battle? But Patrick wasn't very good at the names of famous battles. Impatiently, he dismissed the idea. Cal and his mates would be back soon. Patrick knew he had to get over that wall.

TWO

Patrick leapt, slipped on the lichen-covered brick and fell back into brambles that tore at his bare arms and raked at his T-shirt. Wrenching himself free, he took a running jump at another section of the crumbling stone wall, this time covered with matted ivy rather than slippery moss. He grabbed a handful of the stuff, which came away, dry and dusty in his right hand, but he managed to grasp a thicker strand with his left.

Patrick was tall and lanky, a natural athlete, and he was soon climbing the ivy-covered wall until he reached the top, panting and gasping, pushing back his tangle of fair hair and staring down at the wilderness that had once been a garden.

He paused, gazing at the solid shape of the old house, three storeys high, with attic windows that looked like eyes. The sheer bulk of the place was overpowering.

Like the garden wall, the outside of Columbine House was thick with ivy, and for a moment Patrick wondered if the stuff could have got inside, filling the rooms with rustling strands.

Soon Patrick began to realise he was a sitting target, straddling the wall in the moonlight. What was he doing? Why was he behaving like a fool, a kid playing games? Hurriedly, he dropped down into what he thought was undergrowth, but when he heard a tinkling crash he realised he'd put one foot through a cucumber frame. Luckily he was wearing boots or there might have been a lot of blood.

Suddenly, Patrick thought of the father he hadn't seen since he was six. A man, tall like himself, with a shock of fair hair, who was hardly ever at home. It was as if his father had barely existed. Patrick's only vivid memory of him was from when he was about six. His father had taken him and four-year-old Declan to a fairground, insisting they went on the flying chairs. Whirling round, so high off the ground, Patrick had screamed his lungs out and Declan had been sick.

'Fancy taking the boys on a ride like that!' Mum had been angry.

'They're no sons of mine if they can't take a risk,' his father had bellowed. And the lifetime of argument between his parents had begun yet again. Could they never agree? Or did they have a secret joy in scoring points off each other? Maybe that was necessary for them both.

For a few moments, Patrick stood amongst the shattered glass of the overgrown cucumber frame, waiting to see if he'd been heard. But the shouting was still dim and distant and he thought he was safe for a while.

Cautiously, he eased his right foot out of the glass and gazed towards the house. No lights had gone on, there was no sign of movement and, for a moment, the building looked like the dark hulk of a moonlit ship.

Treading warily, Patrick stole over the undulating ground, the land rising to what might once have been a lawn but was now a meadow of waist-high grass. Again, he stopped and listened, but nothing could be heard from the dense woodland now, not the faintest cry, and no sign of a chink of torchlight. Were they stalking him? Had they heard that sharp tinkling of glass? He hoped to God they hadn't.

Patrick began to pray. He had prayed all his life as a kind of routine defence against the threatening outside world, kneeling by his bed, saying the Hail Marys and crossing himself vigorously.

'Why do you do all that?' Declan had asked him once, barging into his room as usual, looking for something that wasn't his. It was as if he had some uncontrollable urge to invade Patrick's space.

'It's none of your business.'

'You're a superstitious fool. You don't really believe in God either – you just pretend to yourself.'

'Say that again.'

'You're a fool.'

Infuriated by his younger brother's air of superiority, Patrick would hit him hard or even slap his brother round the face time and again, but Declan never called for their mother.

Now Patrick prayed again, standing in the wilderness, crossing himself under the moon. He imagined the all-comforting figure of his mother in the kitchen, sitting at the table with a mug of tea, reading the headlines of the evening paper and putting the world to rights.

He still went to Mass with her at St Stephen's every Sunday morning at 9.30. Declan never came and Mum had said, 'Let him grow up a heathen then. Just like your father. They'll both go to hell – you see if they don't.' Patrick would see Cal at Mass – regular as clockwork. Cal never missed Mass. But his attendance didn't please Mum either. 'He'll be going to hell-fire, just like his dad, hell-fire for the things they do.'

So, thought Patrick, no one could win. Not with Mum.

Patrick crossed himself again, added another gabbled Hail Mary and began to move forwards slowly and cautiously.

Striding out now, knowing he was going to have to break in, Patrick approached the large, square-shaped shadow of the house and paused, checking the downstairs windows. He was quite a dab hand at burglary; Cal had shown him over a dozen ways to break into other people's homes and lift whatever he could. For the Cause, of course. What else?

Cal had never taken anything for himself or allowed Patrick to do so. All the stolen goods were passed on to Cal's father, Liam, who knew how to dispose of them, to turn the stuff into ready money.

Now Patrick was beside the ivy-covered house, trying to push up a window. The paint was badly cracked, but the catch held and, whatever he did, Patrick couldn't shift it. He tried other windows, but they were jammed tight and probably hadn't been opened in years.

Then he tried the back door and almost overbalanced.

Holy Mother, was the old guy out of his mind, or just forgetful? The door wasn't even shut properly.

Patrick stole inside and slowly closed the door behind him, turning the key in the lock. He made hardly any sound at all. In one sense he felt safe. At least Cal and his mates couldn't creep up on him unawares. But what about the Colonel? He remembered him again, the knotted veins standing out on his thin hands.

Patrick stood still, not wanting to move, getting

used to the dark, trying to make out the jumbled interior of what might be a kitchen. Bulky shapes were everywhere, but he soon realised they were mounds of old newspapers, taking up most of the floor space, piled on chairs and scattered over a long table that was deep in shadow.

There was a pungent smell in the room, a shut-in smell that reeked of cooked meat and something acidic. Like old man? For a moment, Patrick's imagination soared, seeing Colonel Springfield in a dressing gown, a raven on each shoulder, a snake coiled around his wheezing chest. Feeling a bit hysterical, Patrick almost laughed, but he soon began to wonder what on Earth he was going to do next. He hadn't thought any of this through; his only objective had been to get clear of Cal. But Patrick knew Cal would never give up. Only by taking the boat to England could he evade him. So what the hell was he doing breaking into Columbine House of all obvious places? In his absence, Cal could trash his home, do terrible things to Mum and Declan. The dreadful thoughts made him sweat in the mildewed kitchen.

Why had he done it? He'd always been one of the lads and Cal had once been both friend and protector. Now only one thing was certain: Cal would never be his friend again.

•

Treading slowly and softly, his eyes now used to the dark, Patrick reached the kitchen door, which had an old-fashioned brass knob that was cold to the touch.

He stopped and listened and then turned the knob. The door opened slowly and noiselessly when he had thought that it would at least make a creaking sound. But that was the stuff of comic books and mystery stories and haunted houses on TV.

This door was for real.

In front of him there was a passageway and against the wall was an aged bicycle, dusty and covered in cobwebs. Something dark rustled in the gossamer strands and Patrick froze, wondering if a crane fly had fluttered into the heavy web, had been caught by the sticky substance and was now flailing, a captured feast for a hungry spider, or maybe just stored in the web larder.

He shuddered and almost cried out as his hand brushed the sticky folds, but Patrick forced himself to move on. He crept up the passageway to the front door that was studded with coloured glass, dimmed to black and white now as the moonlight streamed through.

There were piles of boxes in the hall and more stacks of old newspapers. Patrick hesitated and listened again. All he could hear was the loud ticking of a clock, but still he stood there, hardly moving a muscle, not knowing what to do. The air seemed to become solid around him and increasingly chilly. Had time frozen over? Then he made a stumbling move forward and saw a half-open door further down the passage.

He moved slowly on and squeezed into the room without touching the door. The curtains hadn't been pulled and the moonlight bathed the surprisingly ordered room in a milky light. The chaos was over. The room was neat and lived in, a whisky bottle half empty on a table by a deep armchair that looked well sat in.

There was a grand piano, walls smothered with bookcases, each book neatly arranged, not a spine out of true, and where there weren't books there were pictures and photographs in what Patrick thought were silver frames. There were more frames on the piano and the windowsill as well as the long low table that stood in the centre of the room.

Patrick tiptoed over to the table. He could just make out the shadow-smudged photographs of a man and a woman, both handsome, both with forced-looking smiles, standing in wedding clothes in a church porch, in bathing costumes on a beach, in leathers on a motorbike, wearing casual clothes in vintage cars, and smartly dressed at formal occasions, like garden parties or solemn dinners. Then, on the piano, there was a simple photograph of a young officer.

Was this the only room the Colonel lived in?

wondered Patrick. There were French windows to one side, opening out on to what he thought was a terrace. He could smell the faint odour of stale tobacco smoke and something else, something sharp, like vinegar. Then Patrick realised that the smell *was* vinegar, for lying on the piano was a plate of tinned tuna, accompanied by liberally doused oven chips. There were a few soggy specimens left, obscene-looking in the moonlight, like fat, white slugs.

Patrick wondered whether he should try to find somewhere to hide. If he was discovered here, the police would be called and his sanctuary violated. If the old man were here on his own, then maybe there was a chance he could stay. But how should he handle it? Threaten the Colonel? Beat him into submission? Although he hadn't been in as many fights as Cal, Patrick knew what it was like to use his fists and boots – not that he particularly wanted to fight, but you needed to be hard in these times. That was the way you got respect. But he didn't see himself attacking an old man. If he was quiet and the Colonel didn't wake till morning, Patrick could slip out again. But where could he go? What would he have gained?

A few hours reprieve?

What was the point of that?

He'd have to go home, or Mum would be out of her mind with worry. And then there was Cal…

There was no way out. He'd better get ready to take his punishment. He'd rather get the beating over than hang around like this. Why didn't he just go back into the woods and give himself up? At least they'd probably beat him before morning came and get him into a hospital. Or would Cal just leave him bleeding in the woods? He could die from loss of blood.

Better to wait.

Better to stay here.

Then he could, maybe, ring Cal and start pleading. They'd been friends for years. Surely he'd understand, take an apology into account? And if Cal decided to spare him, then so would the others. Patrick fingered his back pocket. He still had his mobile and Cal always carried one. He could call him now and negotiate.

Then Patrick's optimism died. He knew Cal of old. He was much harder than anyone could imagine. He wouldn't let him off – not after what he'd done.

Indecisive, Patrick turned back to the piano and the single photograph on which the faint moonlight appeared to focus. The young officer stood stiffly, austere in classic pose, on the steps of a building.

Colonel Springfield. As was. Now a rheumy-eyed old man.

What kind of soldier had he been? Brave and upright? As brave as today's men of violence, whose balaclava-covered faces showed only expressionless eyes as they fired rifle volleys over the coffin?

For Patrick, funerals had become a habit, almost an addiction, for however plain or lavish the Mass was, on these occasions he always felt deeply moved. He was part of the tide of humanity that streamed behind the coffin, walking slowly, expression set, following the slow-trotting of the black horses or the smooth hum of the hearse. To share in the honour of death seemed a privilege then, and inside the church he always felt the same, churning with emotion but, above all, churning with belonging to the Cause, a heady feeling of elation. Nothing could compete. Nobody could compete. At times like, this he belonged to the Cause, but only at funerals.

Patrick knew he wasn't alone in his elation. Not only was the suicide rate drastically down because people had so much to do, but so was illness – the kind of illness that got you off work or school with a sick note.

Death's a bit of a party, Cal had said.

Not if you're dead, Patrick had replied, but he knew what he meant all right. Everyday life was drab and dull, despite the Cause, which only made its presence felt from time to time. An ambush, a car in flames, a shoot-out in the streets – all that stirred his blood, just like the funerals that often resulted from incidents like these. But the dreariness of normal life, the fact that he had no pocket money and the newspaper round paid peanuts, was hard, and hard was most of the time when the Cause was as dead to Patrick as the crane flies in the spiders' larder. He didn't want to steal for the Cause. He didn't want to see men shot down, beatings handed out. Sod the Cause. It was only good for the theatre of the funerals and aggression. That was when the tears came – and the adrenalin.

Mum knew how he felt.

'One day,' she had said, 'we'll go to the sea.'

Declan and Patrick had only seen the waves once.

'One day,' Mum had said, 'we'll go to the fair together.' But they'd never made it – nor would they have had any money to spend at the fair even if they had gone.

'One day,' Mum had said, 'we'll go bowling.'

But that cost money too. And then there was Mum's wheelchair to cope with.

Father Joseph had said, 'We need to form a youth club to keep the young people off the streets.'

But neither Patrick nor Declan nor Cal had had any interest in table tennis.

'To hell with that,' Cal had said. 'The parish hall stinks. I'd rather be on the streets.' And he'd been right. With a bit of luck, there was sometimes an errand to run, a message to be passed, even a warning delivered. Well – all that counted for a bit of extra cash, didn't it? And a bit of excitement.

Patrick tried to shrug away the fact that he hadn't the slightest idea what to do next. Then he surprised himself again. He was incredibly hungry. Why not return to the kitchen and dig around in the cupboards to see what he might find? Anything would do. Suddenly he realised that the condemned man might be about to enjoy a last meal.

He began to walk quickly across the room, knocking into a small table laden with more silver-framed photos that slid on to the floor with a loud clatter.

He froze and listened.

The clattering seemed to take a long while to die away.

Still he listened.

But the silence deepened.

With temporary relief, he tiptoed across the floor to the door of the sitting room and the passageway beyond.

Hesitating for a second, Patrick headed for the kitchen, looking up the stairs that he could just make out in the gloom.

Then, as he crept on, a solid object hit him so hard over the head that he could only see darkness – and then nothing at all.

THREE

Patrick came to, his head splitting with dull pain, lying on his stomach, face buried in the greasy smell of the carpet.

He saw a wet patch in front of him and wondered if that was his blood. Or had he pissed himself? But surely he'd have had to be a contortionist to have done that.

His head ached so badly that he brought his hands to his temples, trying to soothe the ache and failing, but finding more sticky wetness that had to be blood.

Had Cal got him? Where was he? The carpet smelt vile and he remembered he was inside the Colonel's ramshackle home.

In considerable pain, Patrick rolled himself on to his back, only to meet the glaring eyes of an old man.

The Colonel himself. He was holding a saucepan.

Was that the intended murder weapon?

Patrick groaned and the Colonel raised the saucepan again.

'Don't,' Patrick whispered. 'Please don't.' The pain in his head throbbed. 'Don't,' he whispered again, hoping to God he was communicating, but wondering if the old man had even heard him.

'Why not?' the Colonel demanded.

'I'm sorry.' Patrick tried to sit up again, but the pain drove him back to the carpet, curling up, clutching his head, wondering how much blood he'd lost – and how much was still dribbling through his hair.

'You're lucky I didn't shoot you.' The Colonel stood over Patrick, the saucepan still clutched in a veined and shaking hand. 'That's what happens to burglars.'

'I wasn't burgling.' Patrick looked up into the old man's watery blue eyes. He was in pyjamas and a dressing gown, but he had nothing on his feet and this made him look strangely vulnerable.

Patrick tried to make himself feel hard. I could take the old bastard any time, he thought. So there was nothing to worry about, was there, only Cal still out there in the woods, no doubt scrambling over the wall, followed by his henchmen, already sneaking across the wilderness lawn to the kitchen door.

He tried to stand up.

'Don't move.'

'I want to look at my head.'

'What the hell for?'

'To see what damage you've done.'

'I hit you damn hard. I hope I've done a lot of damage.'

'If you have – you'll be in trouble with the police. Real trouble.' The old man gave a snort, and when Patrick looked up again he wondered if the Colonel was on the edge of some kind of fit.

'You're a housebreaker! The police have places for boys like you.' The old man waved the saucepan about, his thin arms sticking out from his grubby dressing gown.

Patrick put up a hand to protect himself as the Colonel raised the saucepan above his head. Was he going to bash him again? Something fell to the floor and Patrick wondered what it was. Then he touched his head again, and when he brought his hand away Patrick could smell something sweet and sticky. Baked beans. He almost laughed and then rolled away as the Colonel let fly again, missing him, maybe deliberately, his skinny arm and the saucepan swinging by his side. The Colonel was breathing heavily now and Patrick wondered if the old man was about to have a heart attack.

'You hit me again—' he began.

'And?'

'I'll be the one to call the police.'

The Colonel gave an angry laugh. 'You've got a bloody nerve.'

'You've got to let me explain.'

'Explain? What explanation could you have for

breaking into my home? You're just a common thief.'

Patrick knew that he wasn't a common thief. He'd broken into people's homes plenty of times, and always with Cal. But Patrick hadn't burgled for the Cause. He'd done it for excitement, for the buzz of living life on the edge.

'I'm not a thief.'

'Then what are you?'

'I was being chased.'

'Don't give me that rubbish!' The Colonel raised the saucepan above his head again and Patrick knew he would use it. He had to think fast.

'My father was shot dead. I'm on the run, for Christ's sake!' he gabbled.

There was a momentary hesitation.

'Bloody liar,' said the Colonel. 'You were after my stuff.'

'I swear to God I wasn't. My dad – he was shot dead tonight. A couple of hours ago.' Was he getting through? Maybe he would if he got even more dramatic. 'Look – what else can I say?'

'Prove it.'

'How?' Patrick hesitated and then plunged recklessly on. 'Why don't you phone the police? They'll tell you soon enough.'

'Will they now?' The Colonel still didn't lower the saucepan. Maybe he wasn't getting through. But how much harder could he try?

'My dad,' Patrick said, unsuccessfully trying to put a sob into his voice. 'They shot him dead and the bastards who did that – they're after me. They chased me into the woods and they were closing in. I got over your wall and the kitchen door was open. Why don't you keep it shut and locked?'

·'The cat. She has to go in and out.'

'That's a damn silly reason for keeping a door open in bandit country.'

'This isn't bandit country.'

'It is where I live.' There was a silence between them and Patrick knew they'd reached deadlock. 'I've locked the bloody door,' he said. 'If those bastards got in here they'd have you as well as me.'

'The police can deal with the lot of you.'

'You can't turn me in!' Patrick yelled at him. 'Not after all I've been through. I want to hide. That's all I need – a place to hide. Only for a while.'

Just when he wasn't expecting the Colonel to hit him, he took another swing and the heavy saucepan connected with Patrick's head again, this time on his temple. The pain was intense and Patrick could feel fresh blood flowing over his ear in a steady stream.

'Don't move,' said the Colonel.

Patrick said nothing. His head was hurting in two places at once, but the new wound was giving him a much sharper agony than the old.

'Holy Mother of God—'

'Don't blaspheme.'

'What?'

'I know your type.'

'And I know yours.' Patrick hand went to the new wound just above his ear. The blood seemed to be pouring out and his pain was deepened by fear. If the Colonel landed him one again he could do for him. Maybe he'd rather face Cal's beating than this. 'Look,' said Patrick. 'You've got to help me.' His voice broke genuinely this time and that angered him.

'Help you?' The Colonel scoffed. 'Why should I help you?'

'You hit me. Twice. I'm bleeding. Badly. Can't you see?'

'It's what you deserve.'

'Then hurry up and ring the police. They'll get me into hospital at least.'

The Colonel paused. He still gripped the saucepan, which now had some kind of substance stuck to the bottom. What was it? Patrick couldn't see in the half-light. Then he decided it was probably more baked beans.

'You'll be done for assault,' Patrick warned.

'Me?'

'You. Or GBH. Maybe for manslaughter if you

don't get me some help.' Was the Colonel getting scared now? Like he was. It was becoming a real battle of wits. 'For Christ's sake—' began Patrick.

'Stop blaspheming.'

'You'd blaspheme if half your head was caved in by a saucepan.'

Now the Colonel was hesitating.

'I feel dizzy,' said Patrick. 'You've got to do something.'

The Colonel appeared to have arrived at a decision. 'Get on your feet.'

'Where're we going?'

'To the bathroom. I've got some knowledge of first aid. But if you try anything I'll hit you again.'

'*Some* knowledge isn't any good.'

'Well, that's all I've got.'

Patrick half rose and felt incredibly dizzy. What the hell was he going to do? Cal could still be out there and if he guessed where Patrick was, he'd be in here like a shot. He wondered what his other options were. The police weren't one of them and there was no point in making a break for it and trying to get home. Cal could pick him up there just as easily.

Cold sweat mingled with the blood on his face and neck. Disorientated and sick, he staggered as he straightened up and clutched at the Colonel's shoulder.

'Get off!' rasped the old man.

'I don't feel good.'

Patrick stood alone, still swaying, but not daring to seek support. The old sod was handy with that saucepan and if he landed Patrick one again it could do for him. Suddenly, Patrick was more deeply afraid than ever. He was caught between two enemies. He had nowhere to go.

'Can you walk to the bathroom?' There was a slightly different note in the Colonel's voice, as if he was beginning to worry even more. Well, he bloody well should.

'Depends how far it is.'

'We're not going on a route march.' The Colonel was testy. 'There's one just down the corridor. You go first. And remember—'

'I know. The saucepan.'

'Don't cause me to use it again.'

'You can be sure I won't.'

The downstairs toilet was as dirty and dingy as the kitchen. There was some kind of fur on the pipes and a damp smell that made Patrick feel even sicker.

'I'm—'

'Let me see. Don't say anything.' The Colonel turned on the light and a naked bulb made everything look bleaker.

'I'm going to be sick.'

'Stand still.'

'I can't.' Patrick went down on his knees in front of the cracked china bowl, put his hands on the lavatory seat and vomited for a long time.

The Colonel stood by him silently, waiting until he was finished, occasionally clearing his throat impatiently, as if he thought Patrick was deliberately playing for time.

But as his shoulders heaved again and again, all Patrick could think of was the back door. Despite the fact he'd locked it, Cal could soon kick the door down. There was no sanctuary. Not anywhere.

At last, Patrick got shakily to his feet.

'Pull down the lid and sit on the lavatory,' commanded the Colonel.

'I need to flush this first.'

The smell of vomit was mixing with the damp and suddenly Patrick knelt down again, his head over the bowl.

'For God's sake,' muttered the Colonel.

Patrick couldn't bring himself to reply as he began to throw up again.

The Colonel stood stiffly beside him until Patrick couldn't bring up any more vomit and only a pale bile ran from his lips.

'Now are you ready?'

Patrick nodded and flushed the toilet. But the

stench of vomit still hung in the hot and humid air, obliterating the smell of damp. He got up slowly from his knees and sat down on the lavatory, conscious of the smallness of the space and the fact that the Colonel was so very near him.

'Bend your head forward.'

He obliged and the Colonel proceeded to examine him by the glare of the naked bulb.

'The bleeding's stopped,' he said after a while.

Patrick said nothing, waiting for further announcements. But the Colonel was silent.

'What's the damage?' asked Patrick eventually.

'There are two cuts. One could do with a few stitches, but that's about the size of it.' The Colonel sounded brisk and uncaring. 'I'm going to put a dressing on.'

'And then?'

'I'm going to call the police.'

'For God's sake, don't do that.'

'Why on Earth shouldn't I? I thought you were keen that I should. You broke into my home.'

'I know that.'

'With intent to—'

'With intent to steal nothing. I needed a place of safety.'

'The police station will give you that, and fix up your wound.'

'They'll go to my house.'

'Of course they're bound to inform—'

'I'm talking about Cal. He shot my dad. Killed him with a bullet in the head.'

There was a long silence.

'You're sure about that?' asked the Colonel eventually.

Patrick detected a note of hesitation in the old man's voice and seized his opportunity.

'Do you think I don't know when my dad's dead?' He forced out a convincing sob and was pleased with its authenticity.

'Are you telling me the truth?'

Patrick took great pleasure in the hesitancy of the old man's tone. He was beginning to convince him and felt a rush of triumph.

'I'm telling you the truth, God help me.'

'Your father was shot dead?'

'Are you going to fix my head properly or do you want me to die in your precious house?'

'You won't be doing that.'

'No?'

The Colonel went to a cupboard in the small toilet and pulled out a large rusty tin.

'Call that a first-aid kit?' spat out Patrick.

'It's all I've got. This is going to hurt.'

'What are you using? A scalpel?'

'Iodine.'

'What the hell's that?'

'A rather old-fashioned antiseptic.'

There was a short delay until Patrick felt a new stab of agony, a burning sensation in his wound that made him howl with pain.

'Keep quiet – or your playmates will hear you.' The old man made light of the problem. When the iodine splashed into the second wound in Patrick's head the pain was worse. But somehow he stopped himself crying out, clutching at the lavatory seat until his knuckles showed white, only whimpering with the pain that was slowly, very slowly, going away.

'Bastard,' he whispered.

'Technically incorrect,' muttered the Colonel, but his tone was lighter and Patrick was getting more confident that, at least, pain and all, he was buying time. 'And don't swear at your commanding officer. You could be on a charge for that.'

'You're not going to use that stuff again.'

'I may have to. I've got to ensure the wounds are clean.'

'You did it. You assaulted me.'

'We can sort that out in court.'

Patrick's painful triumph subsided. Maybe he wasn't getting on as well as he'd thought. He'd have to be careful. The Colonel touched both his open wounds with what felt like cotton wool soaked in acid, making him grip the edge of the toilet seat ever harder, gasping and grunting with the agony of it all.

'Have you finished?'

'I think so.'

'Bloody liar.'

'Shut up and keep still.'

'Please.' Patrick began to plead, not caring about his loss of face.

'It's over.' The comment was terse.

'Jesus.'

'I think the wound's clean enough to bandage.'

While the Colonel cut up a strip of sticking plaster with decidedly rusty-looking scissors, Patrick thought ahead desperately, yet again working out his options. He could try and get home, but that would put Mum and Declan at risk. He could find another hiding place. But where? Wasn't it better to stay put? To lie low? The phrases filtered through his mind like the barbed-wire agony of the iodine. Cal could get into the house so easily and the old man wouldn't be able to cope. But maybe he could hide in here for a while, and if Cal didn't find him he might think he'd gone over the border. He could ring his mother on his mobile and try to reassure her. But everything hinged on convincing the Colonel to let him stay.

'It's God's truth they shot my dad,' said Patrick.

'I can soon check that out. The news will be on the radio.'

'Sure.' He hadn't thought of that. It wouldn't be long before the Colonel was on to him. For a moment he wondered if he should take the old man by surprise and tie him up. But what with? Or should he kill him? The idea beat in Patrick's head. He'd never killed anyone, but there had to be a first time, didn't there? Then he could hide without hindrance.

More pain wracked Patrick's head as the old man stuck on the plaster and then the agony receded a little, leaving him light-headed.

'That's it?'

'For the moment.'

'What now?'

'Stay where you are.'

There was a long silence while the old man stood over him. Through the half-open door of the toilet, Patrick could just see the saucepan that the Colonel had placed on a small table outside in the hall.

'What's going to happen?' Patrick tried to sound as childishly helpless as he could.

'Don't give me that.'

'Give you what?'

'The little boy lost.'

'They killed my father.'

'How am I to believe that?'

'How about trying?'

'You're a glib little sod.'

'Let me tell you what happened.' Patrick's mind was racing. 'We were sitting down to our tea.'

'Who?'

'Me and my brother Declan. And my parents.' Patrick paused, thinking ahead. Then he hurried on, still sitting on the lavatory seat, the smell of vomit hanging in the air as heavy as the night. 'There was a knock at the door.'

'Go on.'

'My dad got up—'

'Wasn't he afraid of knocks at the door?'

'We were expecting my gran.'

'Where does she live?'

'Up the road. At number twenty-three.'

'And your own address?'

Now it was like an inquisition. What the hell was the old fool playing at?

'Nineteen.'

'Which street?'

'Tullamore.'

'I know that. Tullamore's down by the river.'

Patrick was pleased that he'd given his actual address and established some credibility.

'Yes.' He paused and put a break into his voice. 'Dad opened the door.'

'Then?'

'We heard the shots. For a while we didn't move. Then I got up and Dad was lying across the doorstep and there was all this blood. There was so much of it – like a sea, an ocean. Dad was face down. Thank God I didn't see his face.' Patrick paused again and began to sob. In his over-stretched imagination he felt the Colonel lay a hand on his shoulder. In reality, the Colonel did no such thing.

'And then?'

'There was this gunman. He was aiming at me. For a moment, I almost wanted him to kill me. He tried to pull the trigger but something got jammed.' Patrick knew he was getting bogged down and turned his floundering into more sobs.

But there was no reassuring response from the Colonel.

'I ran.'

'Outside?'

'Into the kitchen and out of the back door. I ran like hell.'

'Wasn't there anyone there?'

'No.'

'That wasn't very professional.'

'It would have been difficult. The gardens back on to each other.'

'Do they?'

How well did the old man know Tullamore Street? Patrick wondered. In fact, the gardens didn't back on to each other at all, as there was a small service road at the back. But he pressed on. 'Thank God they'd made a mistake.'

'A mistake?'

'There was no one there.'

'Go on.'

'I ran like hell, through the gardens, vaulting the fences. There were a couple of shots.'

'I thought you said there was no one there.'

'They must have come round.'

'Where from?'

'The front door, for Christ's sake. There's a passage—'

The Colonel's interrogation was getting even more intense. 'My uncle used to live nearby. I don't remember any passages.'

'You weren't looking.' Patrick tried another sob, but it sounded false this time and he began to lose confidence. 'I made my way to the woods. They've been after me ever since.'

'You mentioned a name.'

Too late, Patrick remembered he had done just that.

'Cal, wasn't it?'

'Yes.'

'You've just implied you didn't know the man at the door – the man who shot your father.'

Patrick's head was hurting so badly that the pain was clouding his senses. He was going to be in trouble. He was going to be found out – and his place of temporary safety wouldn't be safe any longer. Then he had an inspiration. 'I got it wrong. Cal was the guy round the back.'

'You said there wasn't anyone round the back.'

'There wasn't. Then he showed up, firing shots. Firing at me. But he missed.'

'I see.' The Colonel was looking down at him and Patrick could see his reflection in the fly-blown mirror over the wash basin, just a little to the right of the toilet. Then Patrick looked away – and so did the Colonel, as if they had shared an intimacy. 'Why was your father killed?'

Patrick wasn't ready for this, but somehow inspiration struck again. 'They thought he was a police informer.'

'An informer—'

'Gave names. For money.'

'No names. No pack drill.' For the first time, the Colonel sounded slightly sympathetic and Patrick felt a surge of hope.

FOUR

'What do you mean?' Patrick asked. 'No names, no pack drill?'

'It's just a saying.' The Colonel sounded tired.

'So what now? Are you going to call the police? Have me arrested?'

'That might be the safest plan for you.' Again, that slight tinge of sympathy.

'OK. Just call them.'

'You'd better come with me. Stand up.'

Slowly, the dizziness returning, Patrick stood up.

'Are you able to walk?'

'I suppose so.'

The Colonel reached down and picked up the saucepan.

'You'll not be needing that again,' said Patrick hurriedly.

'You never know when you might need a saucepan,' replied the Colonel.

Patrick shrugged and the Colonel got behind him, placing a hand on his shoulder as if he were blind. It was a strange feeling, but Patrick suddenly had the impression that he was needed, that he had to guide the old man in some way – even if he was still armed with a saucepan. Patrick felt as if he had become the prodigal son, had come home at last.

The phone was on a small table in the kitchen, covered in dust.

'Sit down where I can see you.'

Patrick sat on the edge of an upright wooden chair while the Colonel picked up the phone. Frowning, he put it down and then picked the receiver up again.

'What's the matter?' asked Patrick.

'Can't get a dialling tone.'

'Maybe you've been disconnected.'

'I pay my bills.' He tried again and again, but without success. Then he replaced the phone and repeated angrily, 'I pay my bills.'

'There must be a fault on the line.' Patrick had his mobile in his pocket and hoped the Colonel wouldn't take it into his head to search him.

'Could be.' The Colonel yawned. 'I could tie you to that chair.' He picked up the saucepan, but Patrick didn't feel threatened. There was something defeated about the Colonel now.

'You could.'

'Would you put up a struggle?'

Patrick pulled himself together. 'Let me stay. I won't take anything.'

'Let you stay?' The Colonel sounded bewildered.

'I need somewhere to hide. I can't go out there.'

'Cowardice in the face of the enemy.'

'Too right.' Patrick grinned at the old man for the first time. His head wasn't throbbing so badly now, but he didn't want to leave the dirty, smelly kitchen that suddenly seemed so much like home.

'I think you'd better hop it,' said the Colonel.

'What?' Patrick felt a sense of shock.

'Go on. Get out and don't come back.' The Colonel turned to face him. He looked old and tired. 'Consider yourself lucky.'

'I don't want to go back out there.'

'I'm doing you a favour.'

'That's not a favour—'

'I could have you for breaking and entering.'

'I want to stay.' Patrick was suddenly desperate. 'I'll sleep anywhere.'

'And murder me in my bed.'

'I won't come near you.'

'I told you to get out.' The Colonel seemed adamant and Patrick was horrified.

'Cal's out there in the woods.'

'With his merry men.'

'They're not very merry.'

'Run. Take cover. Run again.' The Colonel suddenly sounded excited. 'Work out a strategy.'

'I'm not in the army.'

'I thought that's how you people saw it – use see it anyway. At war with the British.'

'I'm not at war with anyone,' protested Patrick.

The Colonel picked up the saucepan and stood over him. 'I'm not asking you to go. I'm ordering you, and I don't expect to have my orders disobeyed.'

'Please let me stay.'

The Colonel waved the saucepan threateningly and Patrick stood up. 'I'm going,' he said.

The moon had disappeared behind a bank of clouds and the woods were pitch dark. Patrick had lost all sense of direction.

Would it be possible to find a hiding place out here and then walk to the border? His Uncle Conran lived in Dublin, and although Dublin was miles away he might make it somehow. There was nowhere else to go and he certainly couldn't return home, so he had to head for the border. For the first time in a long time Patrick felt childish tears pricking at the back of his eyes.

Forcing himself to move on, he began to edge his way cautiously through the woods, which he soon found were thicker and denser than before. What he had originally hoped was a path quickly petered out.

The pain in his head got worse and Patrick came to a stop, glancing behind him regretfully at the shadowy bulk of the house, unlit, almost seeming to crouch in the woods as he was, looking as vulnerable as he felt. But the house didn't have to be that vulnerable. He and the Colonel could have barricaded the doors and windows, turned the old place into a fort where he might have hidden for a few days until Cal had given up the chase.

Patrick stood in the undergrowth and saw Cal and himself and the other guys playing football in the recreation ground, roller skating at Blades Rink, swimming at the municipal pool, until their work as runners began. Delinquency was part of the Cause, part of the scheme of things, part of the war. Old habits die hard and anything went in war-time.

Why hadn't the Colonel's phone worked? Because he was a clapped-out old madman of a recluse with a telephone that had been cut off for months, possibly years? Or had Cal cut the line? The thought came into Patrick's mind and stayed. After all, it was an easy enough precaution to take.

But if Cal *had* cut the line, they must have guessed where he was and were tracking him even now. Cal and Roy and Seamus and Ryan and Connor. Friends who had turned overnight into enemies. Patrick remembered Connor's high-pitched giggle and shuddered.

Something moved in the bushes and Patrick froze,

hoping the sound had come from some small animal. Then he thought he heard a sound from a thicket and he froze again. But still nothing happened.

Patrick turned and, finding a gate in the wall he hadn't seen before, began to retrace his steps to Columbine House. Standing on the weed-covered drive he saw the path he'd previously followed as the moon swam out from behind the clouds.

Patrick gazed up at the house yearningly. Couldn't he find somewhere to hide here? A garden shed? Wouldn't it be better to lie low for a while and *then* make for the border? Of course he ought to call Mum, but he didn't want to draw attention to himself – even if he whispered into his mobile.

Regretfully, Patrick turned his back on the house and then hesitated. If he returned and begged, maybe the old man would relent. But he was equally sure he wouldn't – and there was always that saucepan. Not that he couldn't get it off him...

As Patrick walked back up the drive he saw movement in the wilderness of waist-high grass.

Boys and girls come out to play,

The moon is shining bright as day—

The old nursery rhyme rattled about in his head and Patrick was surprised. He hadn't thought about it in years. When he was a kid he'd read the lines in a school book and had felt scared. God knows why. A teacher had told him what the rhyme was about, but he couldn't remember what she'd said. Now what was the rest of it—

Patrick froze. He was sure he could hear sounds from the thicket. But weren't the scurryings just small animals? Wasn't that a dry cough though, or could it be the distant bark of a fox? Then something rose and took shape like a spectre in the moonlight.

It was Cal.

There were other shadowy figures behind him and Patrick muffled a cry of terror. Yes – they were here. And yes – they had found him.

Holy Mary, Mother of God, they were rising out of the long grass like wild animals.

'You bastard,' said Cal as he came out of hiding.

For a few terrible moments Patrick couldn't move, as if he were rooted to the drive. His heart thumped painfully. Then his limbs began to work and Patrick took off, running as fast as he could through a stone arch into the back garden of the house, which was as overgrown as the front. They'd split up, he could be sure of that, and they'd come at him from both sides. He had to get back into the house.

Losing them again, Patrick ran as fast as he could, plunging through the undergrowth, leaping over a wall and up the path.

Then he began to rattle at the back door handle.

This time it didn't turn.

Terrified, he battered and thumped again and again, calling out, seeing Cal coming round the corner, wrenching at the handle. Suddenly the door gave way and Patrick rolled over on the kitchen floor and then struggled up, locking the door again. Had the Colonel heard him? Panic surged. Of course he had.

'Stay where you are.'

At first, Patrick thought the old man was carrying a gun, but in the shadowy light he realised he was holding a walking stick. It would do less damage than the saucepan anyway.

'They're after me. They're out there.'

'So I saw.'

'Where from?'

'My bedroom window.'

'Sentry duty?' asked Patrick.

'Surveillance.'

It was as if they were allies. What could have brought about this sudden change?

'Will you help me?'

'Yes.'

Patrick was staggered. 'They'll try to get in,' he warned.

'So we need to repel boarders.'

'How come you want to help me?'

'I've been thinking.'

'What about?'

'Maybe you're a soldier after all.' The Colonel's hand shook on the stick. 'We could barricade the doors – and the windows.'

'We don't have the time,' said Patrick. He was astonished by this change of tack. Astonished and suspicious. 'They're out there now. They could be in here at any moment.'

For the first time, Patrick remembered that he had not thought of the Colonel's welfare. Well, why should he? He'd attacked him with that damn saucepan and his head still hurt. But why hadn't Cal and the lads pushed their way in yet? Were they playing a waiting game – just to wind him up?

'They'll need to regroup. Let's start on the downstairs windows.' The Colonel sounded experienced and confident, as if he knew exactly what was going on, as if he could fix everything for him.

'What are we going to use?'

FIVE

After a while, Patrick realised that the Colonel's idea of repelling boarders was going to be hopelessly ineffective. Several of the windows in the house were broken and the catches were either loose or covered with so many layers of paint that they couldn't be opened at all. There was that advantage at least, thought Patrick dismally. But Cal would simply smash the glass.

Between them, he and the Colonel tried to pick up a mattress, damp and mildewed, to barricade one of the broken windows. But it was hopeless, for although Patrick could hold one side, the old man was too weak to lift the other.

'This is useless,' said Patrick, still trying to work out why Cal hadn't begun his raid already.

'Why?'

'We need to barricade ourselves into one room.'

'I've got a better idea than that.' The Colonel sounded excitable and out of control, which wasn't exactly reassuring.

'What?'

'The cellar. It's inaccessible from outside.' But the Colonel's original authority had gone. He sounded panicky, as if he wasn't thinking clearly.

'How's that?'

'Comes off the kitchen. The exit was bricked up a long time ago. Used to flood.'

'Why didn't you tell me that before?'

'Memory's not what it used to be.' He sounded apologetic.

'Cal could burn the house down,' said Patrick. 'We'd be trapped.'

'They're not terrorists, are they?'

'For God's sake—'

'Just a bunch of kids.'

'Let's get down to that cellar.'

Then there was the sound of breaking glass.

They both stumbled into the sitting room, the Colonel beginning to wheeze badly. Patrick saw Ryan with one leg over the sill, picking at the glass, while behind him Cal swore loudly. Outside he could hear Connor's giggle.

Patrick ran at Ryan, fists clenched, but he was inside now, standing by the window, staring straight at him. Ryan was overweight and out of breath, but he was still a formidable figure and Patrick hesitated.

'Get out of my house!' yelled the Colonel, brandishing his walking stick.

For a moment, Ryan took his eyes off Patrick,

distracted by the spectacle of the gaunt old man in the ragged dressing gown hobbling towards him, and that was his undoing. Patrick kicked Ryan in the groin and he doubled up, falling on to the dusty floor, his mouth almost comically open, knees drawn up.

Cal was next to try to get over the sill, but was slowed by the jagged shards of broken glass that Ryan had been trying to remove. With an angry roar of rage, the Colonel lunged at Cal and caught him across the face with his stick, putting as much strength into the blow as he could.

Cal began to howl with pain as blood surged from his nose, spurting through his fingers.

Patrick gazed at him in dismay, knowing that whatever Cal had planned to do to him would now be doubled. All Cal had to do was to torch the house and if they were in the cellar they'd be suffocated before being burnt to a crisp…

Patrick looked down at Ryan, who was lying on his side, his legs drawn up to his chin. Then he saw Cal, his face streaming with blood, being pulled back out of the window by his comrades. He vanished from sight, but the howls of pain redoubled as his arms and legs came into contact with the shards of broken glass.

Patrick looked across at the Colonel with respect. He was still an active soldier. There could be no doubt about that.

Ryan, who had been gasping, now lay silent, gazing up at the ceiling. Patrick moved towards him, standing by his side, checking the window again to make sure that none of the others were trying to get in. He could hear Cal bellowing, full of vengeance.

'I'll get that old bastard if it's the last thing I do!'

Ryan struggled to his feet and backed away. 'You're dead,' he said to Patrick. 'You're dead.' He ran to the window and tried to vault out, forgetting the shards of glass. Ryan let out a scream and held up a bloodied hand. Then someone hauled him through and Patrick and the Colonel listened as Ryan continued to scream in the darkness below. A moment later, Patrick heard Connor's high-pitched giggle, dim and distant, as if in retreat.

'We can't go down in the cellar,' began Patrick, gazing at the Colonel. The old man just stood there, wheezing and looking shaken, as if he'd only just realised what he had done, the damage he'd inflicted. Once again, Patrick's confidence in the Colonel evaporated.

'They'll regroup,' the old man muttered.

'Of course they will. Where can we go?'

'There's the summer house by the lake. It's all overgrown.' Then he paused. 'Of course—'

'What do you mean, of course?'

'There's a place – a private place of mine.'

'Where?'

'I'll show you.'

'Let's go.'

'We'll need supplies.'

Patrick looked at the Colonel in amazement. One moment he was an old man, shocked and indecisive. The next, although somewhat tottering, he was back in command. But Patrick still didn't know why he'd changed his mind.

'Wait a minute.'

'We don't have time,' snarled the Colonel.

'Why are you helping me? Only an hour ago you threw me out.'

The Colonel stared at him thoughtfully. 'Nothing happens here,' he said brusquely. 'Now it is – and, besides, I'm beginning to believe you.'

The Colonel opened the back door and suddenly gripped Patrick's arm, making him flinch. 'We don't know where the hell they are.'

'No,' said Patrick miserably. 'We don't.'

'I'm going to do a reconnaissance. It's not that far to the summer house, but it would be a disaster if they saw us.'

'They'll look everywhere. They're not idiots. Once they've checked the house they'll widen the search. And a summer house… Well – it's kind of obvious, isn't it?'

'I told you – it's almost totally overgrown.'

'Even so—'

'And, like I said, there's something else. A little extra. A bit of a plus factor.'

'What do you mean?'

'I'll tell you later. Anyway, you'll soon see. Let me go and check out your friends.'

'They *were* my friends. But they're not now.'

'I'd noticed that,' said the Colonel drily. 'I'm hoping they're regrouping round the front. Licking their wounds. That kind of thing. Let me see if the coast is clear.'

'You can't go out there,' said Patrick feebly, but the Colonel simply pushed him out of the way and headed for the back door, releasing the bolt and tucking his walking stick under his arm.

Patrick crept back to the broken window and gazed out at the front garden. He could see a group of shadowy figures. One of them drew back and Patrick saw that they were huddled round one of their number, recognisable by his shape as Cal. He wondered if his nose was broken.

Then Patrick hurried back to the kitchen and met the Colonel returning through the back door, wheezing and with a triumphant grin. 'There's no sign of the enemy. They must have retreated.'

'They're out the front.'

'So what are we waiting for?'

Patrick hesitated.

'I *said*, what are we waiting for? There's no time to collect provisions. Besides, there may be some in the crypt.'

'The what?'

'Shut up and do as you're told.' The old man dragged at Patrick's arm. 'Move, damn you,' he spluttered.

As he stumbled across the moonlit lawn Patrick was more tense than he had ever been in his life, sure that at any moment Cal and the lads would give chase.

But there was no sign of anyone, unless they were hiding in the bushes, waiting to spring out.

Patrick's heart pounded and his throat was so dry he could hardly swallow as the Colonel dragged him towards what looked like a thick shrubbery. The old man was wheezing, but he was also going at quite a pace.

Letting Patrick go, the Colonel plunged into the bushes and disappeared. In panic, Patrick followed, pushing his way through but finding resistance and losing his bearings.

'Here!' Again his arm was grabbed and again

Patrick was surprised by the strength of the grip. 'This way.' He was pulled through some more bushes, which badly scratched his face and sent thorn fingers into the sticking plaster on his head. The wounds began to hurt again. Badly.

'For Christ's sake – slow up.'

'*Move!*'

'You're scraping me to bits.'

Pushing on, they finally arrived at a small tumbledown building. The Colonel produced a torch from his dressing-gown pocket and shone the weak beam on rotting wood and broken glass. 'The summer house,' he said proudly.

'We're going to shack up in here?' Patrick was horrified. Was the old man really crazy? Cal would find them in seconds.

'You're in for a surprise,' said the Colonel mysteriously, and pushed open the door.

Patrick cautiously stepped over the threshold while the weak torch beam travelled over ancient garden tools and broken seed boxes.

But the Colonel had gone down on his knees and was pulling at something in the floor. With a gasp, he opened what appeared to be a trapdoor.

'I haven't been down here for a while, so the handle's got a bit rusted up.'

'What the hell are you on about?'

'You'll see.' The Colonel stiffly got up, turned round and began to descend a ladder. Feeling his way down behind him, Patrick did the same, instinctively pulling the trapdoor closed above them.

'What's this?'

'The crypt.'

'How come?'

'There was a family chapel here, but it burnt down. So they built a summer house over the top of the crypt. But it's still a place of sanctuary and it's got candlelight.'

Sanctuary. The word had a holy feel. Had he really reached safety at last?

Wheezing slightly, the Colonel lit a candle, and in the dim light Patrick saw a circular space built of dark brick with a stone floor. A brass candlestick on an altar held the lighted candle, and above the altar was a photograph, the image too dark to make out.

'They'll never find us here,' said Patrick in hopeful delight.

'Though we've got to come out some time.' The Colonel sounded depressed.

'What about food?'

'I may have a few supplies. And I know I've got drink.'

Patrick went across to a rickety-looking cupboard that he hadn't noticed before. Inside were a bottle of

Scotch, almost full, four tins of corned beef, a box of biscuits and a packet of matches. There was even a can opener.

'Why do you keep all this down here?'

'I used to come here a lot. Spend a couple of days maybe.'

'What for?' Patrick gazed at him blankly.

'To pray. To think.'

'What about?'

'The past.' The Colonel paused. 'I've got a long past, you know.'

'To think about?'

'To worry about.'

'Why worry?'

'Thereby hangs a tale.' The Colonel went over to the cupboard and grabbed the whisky. Opening the bottle, he took a long draught, not offering any to Patrick. Then, putting the bottle back into the cupboard, he went and sat in a sagging armchair, which had its back to the altar and the dark picture Patrick still couldn't make out. 'I'm sorry there's only the one chair, but age must have its comforts – and its privileges.'

Patrick sat cross-legged on the cool hard stone.

'How's your head?' asked the Colonel.

'Sore.'

'I'm sorry I had to do that. But for all I knew you

could have been out to murder me in my bed.'

Patrick felt terribly tired; suddenly all he wanted to do was sleep. His eyes flickered and with an effort he said, 'I'm OK. It's not hurting so much.'

'We should change the dressings in case some dirt from those bushes has got in. But I'm afraid I haven't got a first-aid kit down here and we could be under siege for a while.'

'They could damage your property.'

'What does that matter? I'll be dead soon.'

'What about your family?'

'I don't have one. I'm the last of the line.'

There was a silence between them.

Then the Colonel said, 'I'm going to get some sleep.' He paused. 'Seems unfair.'

'What does?'

'I've taken the only chair.'

'It doesn't matter.'

'There's a couple of blankets under this cushion.' The Colonel slowly rose to retrieve them. Then he handed the blankets to Patrick who began to wrap them round himself. The Colonel sat back with a sigh. 'Get that candle out.'

Wearily, Patrick unwound the blankets, got up, pinched the flame with his fingers and plunged the crypt into darkness. There was a strong smell of earth and the only sound was the Colonel's wheezing.

Patrick felt a crane fly brush his cheek, with the added menace of its feathery legs. He flinched and gave a cry of disgust. The thing must have followed them in.

'Now what?' asked the Colonel testily.

'Crane fly.'

'What?'

'Daddy-long-legs. I can't stand them.'

'For God's sake, man, what's a flying insect against a shooting party?'

'They revolt me.'

'Grin and bear it.'

'My brother, he loves the things.'

'Good for him.' The Colonel was brisk.

'He thinks they've got a secret language.'

'Is the lad daft?' The Colonel yawned.

'No.' Patrick was firm. 'Declan has an imagination, that's all.'

'Is that how he protects himself?'

'Imagination isn't protection,' said Patrick. 'It's just something you have – or don't. The crane flies don't live long – they get caught in spiders' webs. Hundreds of them.'

'So much for their secret language. Doesn't help them warn each other off.'

'On our estate everyone talks. That's how the enemy moves in.' Patrick paused. 'But Declan and I, we have another language. A secret one.'

'You're talking rubbish. Get some sleep.'

'We don't talk about the Cause.'

'Then what *do* you talk about?'

'Peace. It's what Mum wants. What most of the women want if they're honest, she says. But we have to keep it secret. If Cal understood our language he'd kill us. The Cause – it's a religion to him.'

SIX

Patrick dozed, dreaming of Declan. 'There are no webs in my room,' his brother was saying. 'I don't allow them to spin webs in here.'

Spinning – like flax. Now Patrick was spinning, the web circling about him until it stretched over the surface of the whole world. He was in Cal's web, enmeshed in its sticky folds. Something was heading towards him. Something black and hairy. But just before the spider pounced, Patrick woke to the sound of breaking glass and a burst of swearing. Then he heard a thudding of heavy boots.

The Colonel put a finger to his lips, and they both waited apprehensively.

Wasn't the trapdoor incredibly obvious? Patrick's heart began to hammer again. There was more breaking glass, swearing, and then silence.

After a while, the Colonel whispered, 'They're in retreat – a tactical withdrawal.'

'They might still be there. Could they hear us?'

'No.' The Colonel sounded too confident.

'What about your house?' Patrick whispered. 'They could—'

'To hell with that. I can live down here. I may

even die here.'

'Why?'

'I can smell earth. I find the smell of earth very comforting. Reminds me of my campaigning days.'

'Have you always been in the army?'

'No. Stayed on after 1945 to supervise the laying down of arms and the re-establishment of national borders in Europe. Came out in 1950.' The Colonel barked out the information as if he were talking to a senior officer. Patrick felt an unexpected thrill of companionship, of being comrades-in-arms.

'Have you ever been married?'

'She was a sweet girl.'

'What was her name?'

'Sandra.'

'Do you have a family?'

'We never had children. I regret that.'

'What have you done since 1950?'

'Is that any of your business?' The Colonel suddenly sounded peevish. 'Get me that bottle of Scotch. I need to sleep.'

Patrick got up stiffly, retrieved the bottle and gave it to the Colonel. He unscrewed the top again and took such a long swig that Patrick thought he'd choke.

But he didn't. 'I'll hang on to the bottle for a bit.'

'You going to drink the lot?'

'That's none of your business either.'

'That photograph. Is it any of my business?' Patrick looked up into the darkness that was the altar.

'Oh, that.'

'Well? Can I take a look? Let me borrow the torch.'

'Why not.' The Colonel picked up the bottle again and Patrick went over to the altar, switching on the beam. In the dim light he could just make out that the photograph was of a youngish man. 'He wasn't much older than yourself,' said the Colonel.

'Who is he?'

'A soldier.' There was a long pause and then the Colonel continued quietly. 'Actually, I saved his life.'

'Is he still alive?'

'Maybe.' The Colonel took another long pull of the Scotch.

'Do you see him?'

He took another swig and didn't reply. Patrick wondered if he were going to finish the bottle. But he wasn't bothered. He'd seen enough boozing in his time.

'Why have you got his picture down here? Over the altar?'

'To remind me.'

'What about?'

'That at least I did something worth doing.'

'In the war?'

'Yes.'

'You rescued him – like you've rescued me.'

'Sort of.' The Colonel sounded evasive.

'Well – are you going to tell me the story?' Patrick was suddenly wide awake. He shuddered as he looked up at the walls and imagined the dark matted webs. He grabbed the torch and switched it on and off again.

'What are you doing?'

'Can't we have some light for a bit?'

'What about your playmates? They could come back and see the light under the floorboards.'

Patrick switched the torch on again and quickly scanned the webs. No spiders as far as he could make out.

'Get that damn torch out. Give it to me.'

Patrick handed the torch back. 'Are you going to tell me the story?'

'What are you on about?'

'The story of that bloke in the photograph. What happened?'

'Well, if you really want to hear—' The Colonel sat up in his chair.

'I do.'

'Don't interrupt then.'

Patrick sat back on the floor cross-legged and leant against the cool bricks of the wall. 'I won't,' he said.

SEVEN

'I was in France in Normandy at the beginning of the war,' began the Colonel. He spoke confidently and with easy authority, as if he were no longer an old, drunken man, but much younger – a real professional. 'I was a lieutenant then – in charge of a small platoon – and we were trying to make the Dunkirk beaches where we hoped we'd get evacuated. On the way we managed to hide in a village called Arnay. There were fourteen survivors, including myself, and we'd already been in Arnay for a couple of nights. The French had been good to us and had hidden us in the crypt of the church. Now I'm hiding again, with only one companion, in a French crypt without a church. But we're not many miles from Arnay – not as the crow flies. By the way, I've never asked you your name.'

'Patrick.'

'My name's Springfield. Ernest Springfield.'

'I know. You came to our school. The Head was overjoyed to get a war hero to open the fête.'

The Colonel stared at him suspiciously, as if he were wondering if he was being sent up, and then abruptly continued his story, returning to his easy authority. 'The crypt was a perfect safe haven and there were similarities to our present hiding place. No visible steps down, only a trapdoor that was just like the one we have here. That's why I was so pleased to find this sanctuary – uncannily similar to the crypt in that Normandy village all those years ago.

'When Sandra and I first bought Columbine House, I could hardly believe what we'd found under the summer house – it was as if the crypt at Arnay had somehow been transported to Northern Ireland. At first I found the coincidence unsettling, as if the past had become the present and was trying to catch up with me. But later I came to be pleased in a strange sort of way, and when Sandra died I began to spend a lot of time down here. Remembering.

'Before we holed up in the crypt at Arnay, we'd been hiding up in another village a few miles away. While we were there, my sergeant, Jack Cox, told me about a dream he'd had. He'd dreamt that he was walking down the main street of the village towards a children's playground near the town hall. It was early on a summer's afternoon and all the buildings had been shelled. There wasn't even a bar open and most of the population were living in the ruins of their homes. Standing on the steps of the town hall was a cloaked figure with a scythe, and when Jack got nearer he saw that he was staring straight into the eyes of Death.

'"I've got an appointment with you," said Death.

'"Sure as God you haven't," said Jack, and ran like hell in the opposite direction. When he looked back, Jack saw that the steps of the town hall were empty. Death was no longer waiting for him. He had suddenly broken his appointment.

'A couple of days later, we were able to move on to Arnay where we were hidden in the crypt. Jack looked devastated the next morning, just when we'd all had a reasonably good night's sleep.

'"What's going on?" I asked him. "You look terrible."

'"I had a dream about Death, sir," he told me. "Again."

'I told Jack to get a grip on himself, but nothing could stop him telling me about his dream.

'"I was walking towards the church steps, but this time here in Arnay," he told me. "There was this cloaked figure standing at the top and as I got closer I saw he was holding a scythe. Death again, I thought. Oh well, I avoided him last time and I've told him I'm not keeping any appointments. No chance. But as I stood staring up at him, Death said, "You've got an appointment with me, haven't you?"

'Jack replied, "I don't keep any appointments with you." He was about to turn away when he realised that he had to go past Death into the church to get to the crypt. "And I'm not keeping any appointment now," he added. But as Jack pushed Death aside he felt a cold hand on his shoulder.

'"This *is* your appointment," said Death. "I've been waiting for you here in Arnay."

'Jack hurried into the church and then woke up, trying to shrug off his dream, but not succeeding. "Death's not to be listened to," I told Jack, and he grinned and nodded, but I knew I hadn't convinced him.

'Anyway, as I said, we spent a couple of nights in the crypt at Arnay, all fourteen of us, and the French looked after us. The village was right off the beaten track and the Germans, who had passed through a couple of times, seemed unlikely to come back. But on the third day German reconnaissance planes flew low over Arnay and we were anxious. The French told us to stay in the crypt and not wander around the village — and that was pretty sound advice. But we knew we had to leave Arnay sometime, to try and make the beaches at Dunkirk.

'Meanwhile, we were living the life of Riley, with rations of butter and bread and eggs and cheese, lots of fruit and tomatoes, and as much red wine as we could drink. But we were always conscious that if we didn't move on we might be trapped in the village until the end of the war — and who knew when that would be. So we *had* to leave. The question was — when?

'The longer the Germans stayed away, the more I thought we should take to the road. But I also knew that once we got back into the thick of things, there was more chance we'd run up against a German patrol and be taken prisoner.

'As I said, there were fourteen of us, and the men came from a number of very different backgrounds. I was a professional soldier, and we also had a dentist, a solicitor, an undertaker – we were always joking that he could turn out to be the most useful chap out of all of us – a butcher – enough said about him – and even a bloke who'd been a tango dancer. There was this real wide boy, and amongst the younger men a chap who must have lied about his age when he signed up. His name was Tom. I'll always remember Tom. He was a nervous lad, so I suppose lying his way into the army had just been a rather romantic thing to do. In reality, we'd seen a lot of action, and the death toll had really devastated Tom. His nerves were hanging together by a thread, but the crypt was a real boon and Tom was gradually getting back a little confidence. So I decided to spend another night there. I'd also been trying to think of a way of disguising the platoon and had a vague idea of passing them off as farm labourers. But if this was to work I had to have the co-operation of the local farmers.

'The man I'd got closest to in the village was the

doctor – Henri Dupois. He'd patched up a couple of our lads' wounds and Dupois and I had several long talks about the war and how he would like to help us. He soon pooh-poohed my idea of passing the men off as farm labourers – in fact, he seemed vastly amused by the idea. Dupois suggested we'd be better off as a gang of French railway workers, and that if we kept close to the tracks and had some authentic equipment, then at least we'd have a chance of making the coast without getting picked up.

'He knew there'd been a lot of recent sabotage on the railway lines by the French Resistance and that the Germans were anxious repairs should be made as quickly as possible – despite the fact that there could be more sabotage.

'Henri brought some kit over – boiler suits that were made in a local factory – and we changed into them, feeling pretty stupid, but hopeful all the same.

'Then something happened. Just as we were about to spend the third night in the crypt, we heard the sound of engines outside and when Tom went up into the church to look through the window he saw trucks marked with British Field Security insignia roaring round the square. One of the trucks had stopped at Dupois's and a Field Security officer was talking to him on the doorstep.

'"Dupois is looking worried," Tom told me.

"Maybe Field Security's got bad news."

'Of all units, I thought it strange for Field Security to have turned up in the square at Arnay. They must be looking for someone – maybe a British soldier – but why? At a time like this when the French had laid down arms, the country was occupied by Germany and a mass evacuation of British troops was underway. Why was it so important to look for some villain now?

'Once Tom had rejoined us I cautioned the platoon to lie low and not attempt to find out what was going on.

'"But they'll have news, sir," Jack Cox, my sergeant, argued. "And it could be important. They might be able to help us escape. Surely we've *got* to approach them."

'Slowly Jack began to convince the men, but he couldn't convince me. For some reason I was wary, and I gave the platoon orders to stay where they were. After all, why hadn't Dupois come straight over to fill us in, or even brought Field Security to our aid. When I went up into the church to take a cautious look out of the window, I saw that the truck was still parked outside Henri's house, while a member of Field Security was waiting in the passenger seat, a rifle cradled on his lap. Three more trucks, each with two members of Field Security inside, were parked opposite the town hall.

'No one else was in the square and the houses had a tense feel to them, as if their inhabitants were peering cautiously out, trying not to be seen, just like I was.

'I was at the top of a small wrought-iron staircase that led to a room full of religious reading material. From this position, without being seen from outside, I could see the square through a small, round window.

'"What are we going to do, sir?" asked Jack Cox who had just joined me.

'"Nothing."

'"You mean we're not going to make ourselves known to them?"

'"Not at the moment."

'"Why not, sir?"

'"I just don't think it's advisable," I said guardedly.

'"I think you're right, sir," said Jack unexpectedly, gazing down at the trucks again. "There's something going on – and I don't like it."

'"What do you mean?"

'"I was stationed at Aldershot and I saw the trucks Field Security used."

'"What the hell are you on about?" I snapped irritably.

'"All I'm saying is – they're not the type of trucks they use."

'"Do they all have to be the same?"

'"They're not the standard model."

'"Aren't there other models, for God's sake?"

'"Not for Field Security there aren't."

'Jack ran a small garage somewhere in the Forest of Dean and was an expert on anything that ran on four wheels and even two. But I didn't want to hear any more from Jack because by now I was trying to convince *myself* there was nothing wrong. Yet, at the same time, I was still wondering why British Field Security had driven into this remote village and why one of them was spending so much time in Dupois's house.

'"Let's get back into the crypt," I said, and Jack and I hurried down the wrought-iron staircase and lifted the trapdoor.

'I sat down and closed my eyes, but couldn't relax. If there was something wrong, what was it? Jack kept going on about the truck not looking right.

'I called Tom over to me. "Go and check the square from the reading room window every half hour. I want to know how long Field Security stay." But what I really wanted to know was what was happening in the Dupois house.

'I eventually dropped off to sleep until Jack shook me awake. "What is it?"

'"They've gone."

'"Who?" I demanded, still half-asleep.

'"The trucks."

'"What about the member of Field Security who was in Henri's house?"

'"He's gone too."

'"I think we should do a recce – check out that Henri is all right. I'd really like to know what they were doing there."

'"Same here, sir," said Jack. He still looked uneasy. "Shall I go across?"

'"OK, Jack. But be quick." And then I added, "And for God's sake, be careful."

'I went back up into the reading room and watched as Jack left the church, walked across to Henri's house and knocked on the door. He waited some time before the door slowly opened, but I couldn't see who was there. Henri was married with three children and his house was one of the largest in the village.

'Jack disappeared inside and I waited – and went on waiting. Jack didn't appear again and I stood there, as if for an eternity. Still he didn't reappear.

'"What's going on, sir?" asked Tom, who had joined me.

'"Nothing much," I replied. "That house is getting to have a spell on it. Anyone who goes in doesn't come out." I was trying to joke, but not succeeding, staring across the square at the large grey building with the black front door and open shutters. "I never thought Henri was that long-winded."

'Tom and I waited for a very long time, but Jack didn't come out and when I looked at my watch I realised that over half an hour had passed. "This," I remember muttering, "is ridiculous."

'"Shall I nip over, sir?" asked Tom.

'"No. I'll go. I'm sure Henri's giving Jack a drink and they've just got talking. Tell the others I shan't be long."

'As I went down the staircase and towards the main door of the church I thought I heard an engine revving, but the sound quickly faded. Feeling a fool in my boiler suit, as if I were in a very obvious disguise, I walked out of the church.

'I was just about to ring the doorbell when I noticed that Henri's front door was ajar. I hesitated and then slowly pushed it open.

'"Anyone there?" I whispered, and then cursed myself, remembering I was speaking in English, giving myself away to anyone who happened to be about.

'There was no reply.

'Unable to think of the French words I needed, I walked slowly and as softly as I could through the door, still leaving it open.

'Inside there was a curious smell which I couldn't

immediately identify. Then, with shock, I realised that the smell was human excrement. Henri's house was quite old. Had the drains finally packed up?

'I carried on down the corridor. I'd never been in the house before. I'd first met Henri on the steps of the church when the fourteen of us had arrived, battered, dirty and wounded. He'd immediately taken over, showing us to the church and its unique crypt – the ideal hiding place.'

The Colonel turned to Patrick suddenly. 'But it was not as ideal a hiding place as where we are now.' He looked pleased with himself.

'Go on,' said Patrick impatiently. 'What happened next?'

'Henri's house had a long central corridor with doors leading off, and I pushed open each one to reveal a bathroom and then the kitchen, a small study, a consulting room and what looked like some kind of medical store.

'There was a door at the end of the corridor that was slightly open – just as the front door had been. I hesitated, aware that the horrible smell of excrement had intensified.

'I waited and then suddenly moved forward, pushing open the door, shivering.

'What I saw made me almost pass out and then, when the muzziness cleared, I was horribly sick. I stood on the threshold, still unable to believe what I was seeing.

'Henri and his wife were slumped in their chairs at the bloodstained table, but the three children – two girls and a boy – were lying on the floor. The whole setting had the feel of some macabre tableau, as if they were arranged for a photograph.

'Jack was in an armchair.

'All of them had been shot. Some of the shots were neat, but others were more ragged. There was blood everywhere.

'All the lights in the room were switched on.

'I stood there, shaking and incredulous.

'Then I remembered Jack's dream of his appointment with Death. So he'd finally met the Grim Reaper.

'I still stood staring, oblivious of any danger to myself. For God's sake – who had done this terrible thing – and why?

'Then I remembered Field Security. Those trucks aren't right, said Jack's voice in my head. What had he meant? In what way weren't the trucks right?

'The shaking got worse, until it seemed I would never stop. I still stood there, staring at the ghastly spectacle.

'All the corpses seemed to have a slight look of surprise on their faces.

'I turned away, trying to break the grisly spell, realising how much danger I was in.

'But the trucks had gone before Jack entered Henri's house, I thought. Our own Field Security? What on Earth had happened?

'I began to hurry back down the corridor towards the front door. Once outside I was sick again and then ran across the deserted square to the church, up the steps, through the door and across the nave, sprinting even faster now, heading towards the trapdoor to the crypt and hurling myself down the steps to stand trembling in front of the men, unable to speak, unable to put into words what I'd seen.

'"What's the matter, sir?" asked Private Lucas.

'"Is something wrong?" Lance Corporal Harris was gazing at me in mounting apprehension.

'I nodded. "There is something wrong." At last I'd managed to get the words out.

'"What's happened, sir?" asked Tom.

'Slowly, shakily, I began to tell them.

'When I'd finished my explanation, there was a long silence.

'Lance Corporal Harris said, "You know what Jack said."

'"There was something wrong with the trucks. Something wrong about the way they looked."

'Harris nodded and Tom said, "Who were they in the trucks?"

"'I don't know."

"'They weren't Field Security then?"

"'Can't have been. That's why they weren't in standard issue vehicles."

"'Who then?" Tom repeated.

'I shrugged.

"'Did the trucks ever go away, sir?"

"'What?" I looked at Tom impatiently. "What do you mean?"

"'Did they ever go away? I mean, it looked like they did, sir, but the trucks could have gone down the road and parked out of sight. Maybe some of them walked back and waited. They could have seen Jack walking across from the church. Now they know where we are."

'There are thirteen of us now, I thought, and thirteen's an unlucky number.

"'OK." I tried to be decisive. "We've got to get out – get out and keep going."

"'They won't let us do that, will they, sir? They'll be waiting somewhere to ambush us," said Tom.

"'Then we'll shoot our way through."

"'That may not be possible," said the ever-logical Lance Corporal Harris. "We don't have enough ammo."

'"We've got to get going now."

'"I don't think that's possible either, sir."

'"What *are* you talking about, Harris?" I was furious now, completely losing my temper.

'"Listen, sir."

'Now we could all hear the sound of the engines in the square outside.

'"Stay there!" I shouted, and ran up the steps to the trapdoor, across the church and then up to the reading room. The four trucks were back and had parked in a half-circle in the square. The occupants were standing beside their vehicles, rifles in hand.

'One of them had a megaphone, which he put to his lips. "You are surrounded," he announced in a tinny voice. "Come out unarmed and give yourselves up. I shall give you three minutes. That is all the time you have."

'I felt the cold disgust of self-loathing. I should have realised what was going to happen. But Jack's death – all the deaths – had set me reeling, frozen my mind.

'The man's accent was German and I realised how easily tricked we'd been. The Germans were using a Field Security disguise to flush out British troops from the more isolated villages. Why hadn't I thought of such an obvious ploy? Now, as the seconds ticked away, I turned and raced back to the crypt.

'"I'm going to talk to them," I said when I'd explained what was happening.

'There was a murmur of dissent. Someone said, "They'll kill you."

'Then Harris said, "So Jack was right all along. The trucks weren't right. They must be German."

'I nodded impatiently. "I haven't got time for all this. I'm going out to negotiate. Under the Geneva convention they have to make us prisoners of war and we have rights—"

'"Did Jack?" asked Tom. "Did Jack have rights, sir?"

'I avoided his eyes. "I'm going out," I repeated. "Everyone else is to remain here."

'"They'll kill you, sir," warned Harris.

'"Nonsense. I must negotiate the terms of our surrender." I looked at my watch. "I don't have time to hang about." I turned away and strode swiftly to the steps. "I'll be back very soon."

'Twilight was fading into darkness in the square. I had never been so terrified in my life. Maybe Harris was right and they would kill me. Death was certainly having a carnival in Arnay.

'I raised my hands, but was immediately dazzled by harsh spotlights. Mounted on the bonnets of the jeeps, the lights were relentlessly penetrating.

"'I can't see," I said, my arms still raised. "I need to talk, but I must see you.'"

'After a short delay, the beams were lowered and a man in Field Security uniform stepped forward. "Who are you?"

"'I'm Lieutenant Ernest Springfield and I'm in command of the Twenty-second Infantry Platoon."

"'How many of your men are in the church?"

"'Twelve – including myself." As I was now expecting the worst, I instinctively decided to count Tom out. Maybe we could hide him. It was of course a sentimental and essentially stupid idea. What did age matter at a time like this? But I felt as if I'd betrayed them all with my stupidity, my lack of far-sightedness.

"'Where are the others?"

"'Dead."

"'I trust you are telling me the truth, Lieutenant."

'I nodded silently, and then asked, "Who are you?"

"'Oberleutnant Werner Kruger. I am in charge of this search."

"'Search for who?"

"'British soldiers who have not surrendered – and have taken advantage of French protection. This has the most serious repercussions."

"'Is that why you've disguised yourselves as British Field Security?" I sneered.

"'The disguise has been most successful." Kruger sounded very smug.

"'I need to negotiate the terms of our surrender under the rules of the Geneva Convention."

"'The Geneva Convention doesn't apply in these circumstances."

"'Why not?" The coldness in my stomach seemed to reach my throat as I suddenly realised that I was helpless.

"'You put innocent lives at risk. French lives."

"'Is that why you executed Henri Dupois's family?" I realised I had nothing to lose now.

"'We were compelled to do that."

"'You murdered them."

"'They were concealing the enemy."

"'My sergeant was murdered."

"'We obviously interpret the situation differently," said Kruger blandly, and for a moment I experienced a blind rage. But it slid away into the coldness.

'I realised the impasse was growing and that, if I wanted to save the rest of the platoon, I would have to do better than this. As a result, I tried to sound much more confident than I felt.

"'I expect you to take me and my platoon prisoners of war under the terms of the Geneva Convention."

'Kruger smiled, as if he were talking to a child. "'The French need to understand the consequences of harbouring the enemy."

"'I would have thought you had already made sure of that."

"'There must be more."

"'More what?'"

"'Executions."

"'For God's sake, man—" I began as the shockwaves hit me.

"'The French have been harbouring a large number of British soldiers in this area. An example must be made. I intend to execute more French citizens as well as British soldiers."

'I could hardly believe what I was hearing. "This is a massacre," I began, but Kruger shook his head impatiently.

"'We are at war. This is a warning to French citizens not to harbour the enemy."

"'Look, you've already made your point—"

'But the Oberleutnant interrupted. "I do not wish to continue this conversation. How many of your men are in the church?"

"'I told you – twelve."

"'And you said that included yourself?"

"'Yes."

"'Very well – you will be taken prisoner of war, Lieutenant. Your platoon will be executed along with a group of French citizens."

'My mind was racing as he outlined his plan. Wasn't there someone higher up in the German chain of command I could reach?

'"I insist on speaking to your superior officer," I said.

'He shrugged. "Of course. He'll be along. But in the meantime I suggest you round up your men and bring them out of the church with their hands raised. We will need all your weapons to be deposited in the nave of the church."

'My mind was still racing. I'd have preferred to come out shooting rather than surrender and see them executed. But I needed to talk to the men.

'"If there are to be executions, Oberleutnant, I'd rather join my men."

'"That is not your choice. You will be interrogated. You may know troop movements, and, of course, you may know where other British soldiers are hiding."

'"I've no idea. All troops are heading for the beaches, as I'm sure you must be aware."

'"We do not intend to execute you, Lieutenant. Now go and talk to your men."

'"Your commanding officer won't allow—" I broke off, knowing I had already lost the argument.

'"Go and talk to them, Lieutenant."

'I turned away, walking back up the steps to the

church, feeling utterly powerless. What were we going to do?

'Then another thought struck me. Now that we had all changed into boiler suits and were not in uniform, the Germans could more easily ignore the Geneva Convention as to the treatment of military prisoners of war. In other words, they could simply choose not to recognise that we were soldiers. Having seen Jack, the Oberleutnant was probably banking on this, and there was nothing I could do about it as our uniforms had all been taken away by Henri Dupois and destroyed.

'I went in to speak to the platoon, feeling utterly devastated.

'The remainder of the platoon gazed back at me as I gave them the appalling news. At this stage I didn't tell them that I'd left Tom out of the head count. God knows what the others would think. Maybe I'd wanted to protect him because I had no children of my own, because I saw him as a son. But the rest of the platoon would find this ludicrous and each man would probably feel that if someone were to be saved why shouldn't that someone be them. Then I suddenly had an idea.

'"I've got a plan," I began. "There are only eight of them. We should resist."

'"We've got practically no ammo left," said Harris. "Just a few rounds."

'"Then we should go hand-to-hand. We've got bayonets and knives. With a bit of luck some of the French may join us."

'"I doubt that, sir," said Tom.

'"OK," I replied, ignoring him. "So who's volunteering?"

'"What for, sir?"

'The crypt was, as ever, in darkness and I was finding difficulty gauging their reactions. "Half of us should fend off the enemy – the rest should try and make an escape across the fields. It's all a question of who gets the short straw."

'There was an uneasy silence.

'Then Harris said, "I think that's a damn good idea, sir."

'But no one else said anything.

'"Come on," I said impatiently. "They won't wait out there for ever." But I could sense a curious embarrassment, as if no one was going to obey me. Then there was whispered assent.

'I decided to switch on the lights in the crypt and try to find something that would do duty for straws. Eventually I began to rip up the pages of a hymn book, providing six long pieces and seven small. What a fool I'd been about Tom. He would have to take his chances – just like any of us. I must have been cracking up to have thought so sentimentally about him.

'Choosing the straws turned out to be just about the worst experience I'd had, even worse than witnessing the aftermath of the massacre.

'Anyway, to cut a terrible story short, it worked out that Harris, Bryant, Regan, Lucas, Hagan, Turner and Tom got the short straws, and Standen, Billings, Ropley, Herington, Chivers and I got the long. No one said anything or showed any emotion, but I said quietly, "I have to lead from the front, Tom. You went last, so here's my straw for you." At least I had made him go last on the chance that this might happen. He looked stunned, as if he couldn't cope. No one spoke.

'Harris and I then took another few minutes dividing up what little ammunition we had left. When that was done I said, "Go to the back door and just wait until you hear us shooting."

'"Wait a minute, sir," said Harris. "Why wouldn't they guard the back of the church? They'd be fools if they didn't. The Germans have probably already guessed that we're not going to surrender just like that."

'"There aren't enough of them," I said deliberately dismissive. This was their only, small, chance, they had to take it regardless of the risk. I moved towards the stairs, followed by the rest of the suicide squad. I think we all felt incredibly numb, knowing we hadn't had time to think everything through – and didn't *want* to think everything through.

'Then I heard Tom come up behind me. "Excuse me, sir."

'"What is it?"

'"They won't shoot you, will they, sir? I mean—"

'"They will if I start shooting at them."

'"But, you're a senior officer—"

'"Go and join the others," I told him. "And that's an order."

'We filed up the steps, opened the trapdoor and waited for each other. Then half of us began to walk slowly down the nave – and the other half crept over to the back door, crouching down behind the pews.

'The front doors of the church had been swung partly open and the Oberleutnant appeared on the threshold.

'"Drop your weapons," he said.

'But we walked on, with this strange, stiff walk, as if we were dreaming.

'"Where are the other members of your platoon?" he demanded. Kruger was very agitated.

'Still we strode on and the Oberleutnant suddenly ducked out of sight. I swore, realising we hadn't been quick enough. We could have killed him. "Keep going," I said to Harris.

'"What's that rumbling noise?" he asked.

'"Just keep going." Then, after a few seconds, I said, "Now run. Run like hell."

'But as we made the main doors of the church I saw to my horror that a large truck had just pulled in and German soldiers were swiftly climbing out of the back.

'The Oberleutnant was crouching down behind his truck and I noticed that out of the three vehicles, two were missing. The other trucks must have been driven round to the back of the church. Had I gone mad? The others had no chance, whatever we did. But we had to try anyway.

'"Fire!" I yelled at Harris.

'We sprinted down the steps with our rifles blazing and I think we hit some of the enemy. But I could never be sure for they fired back within seconds. Harris was the first to fall, rolling down the last few steps while I ran on as if I were invincible. Then I realised I wasn't, as the first bullet entered my gut and another my chest. I fell on the broken cobbles of the square but felt no pain. The spotlit square darkened and then blackness overwhelmed me.'

EIGHT

Patrick said nothing. Slowly he got up, lit the candle, and stared into the Colonel's eyes. For a second, Patrick wondered if the old man was being totally frank about what had happened, but the Colonel had admitted his mistakes so he couldn't be dressing up his account to present himself as a hero. Nevertheless, Patrick felt uneasy. The account didn't entirely ring true. The Colonel seemed to have missed a few tricks. Too many tricks.

'But you survived.'

'I was badly wounded. I slowly recovered in a military hospital. I don't know why they didn't just finish me off.'

'Because the Germans thought you could give them information – about the troop movements.'

'I knew nothing.'

'They weren't to know that,' said Patrick. 'And Lance Corporal Harris?'

'He died. So did the other five. But the six round the back struck it lucky and got away. Two were captured and the other four made the beaches and eventually got a boat. At least we'd made a little bit of military history.'

'But why hadn't the Germans gone round the back of the church? They *must* have realised your tactics.'

'They were too late,' said the Colonel stiffly.

'But—'

'I told you.' The Colonel was getting bad-tempered. 'They were too late.'

How? wondered Patrick. How could they be too late? But he decided to ask another question instead. 'What about Tom?'

'He made it and I was glad. But I was just sentimental about him. All these years I've thought about Tom – as if he were my son. The son Sandra and I couldn't have.'

'Is that his photograph?'

The Colonel struggled out of his armchair and with some effort lifted the picture down.

'He was too young to die, that's why you looked out for him especially,' said Patrick. 'How badly wounded were you?' he added.

'I spent three months in hospital. Then I was sent to a prison camp for officers in Germany. We were all interrogated intensively.'

'Did you give them anything?'

The Colonel paused, reflected and then shook his head. 'Nothing that was any use to them.'

'And then?'

'I stayed there until the war ended. But afterwards I remained in the army, working in Germany, helping to supervise the laying down of arms, liberating the concentration camps... That was a terrible experience that I don't want to talk about.' The Colonel sank back in his old wreck of a chair, still clutching Tom's picture. He seemed very tired. 'I've told you my story – now you tell me yours.' The Colonel was smiling, as if they were playing some kind of game, as if he were challenging Patrick.

'I don't have one to tell.'

'Of course you do. How your dad got shot. Or would you rather sleep? And cop out of the truth.' The Colonel unscrewed the top of the whisky bottle again and took a long swig. Patrick wondered how drunk he had been when he was telling his story – and how much drunker he was going to get. 'Come on,' said the Colonel. 'I've confessed. Now you have to do the same.'

'I'm not going to have you falling asleep on me.'

'Why should I do that?'

'Because you're pissed.'

'How dare you!' The Colonel was putting on a show of being affronted.

'I dare,' said Patrick.

'I'm listening to every word, and mind you tell me the truth.'

Slowly, and at first very hesitantly, with his head still aching, Patrick began.

NINE

'I've lived round here all my life. The town's always been a dump and we never had any money. OK, so I've been to Dublin a couple of times, and once to the sea. We stayed in a boarding house and this landlady was a right cow.' Patrick paused, wanting to keep track. 'My dad's – he was – a clever man and an honourable one. He could turn his hand to anything. He was busy all the week, but over the weekends we would sometimes take walks over the hills.

'Those were our best times – just him and me. We used to talk about other places, other lands. We were always doing that. Talking – never seeing, never going, but that didn't matter. Dad was magic when he talked about California and Hollywood, Florida and Disneyland. I guess he'd read about them in magazines and books. Dad made me want to read more. Declan always has. I'm good at sport though. Football and curling and ice hockey, and I'm in the school teams for football and for curling. So I'm busy on Saturdays, but Sundays are for walking and talking and hearing stories from Dad, not just about America, but about Africa and India and the East. And then there were the poles. Dad had read lots of books on Scott of the

Antarctic. "Now there was a man," I remember him saying, "who went and fouled things up, but he was a hero just the same." He told me about Scott's diaries and what he'd written at the end, when he was dying. Something about asking his wife to make sure his son got interested in natural history. Scott said natural history was better than games.'

Patrick looked at the Colonel for the first time and detected what he thought was a look of disbelief in the old man's eyes.

'Don't you believe me?'

'Why do you think I don't?'

'I swear to God I'm telling you the truth.'

The Colonel nodded. 'What kind of man was your father?' he asked abruptly.

'I told you – he was an honourable man.' Patrick paused but the Colonel said nothing. He was sitting up now, no longer slumped in the chair, watching him intently. 'There was this guy called Rafferty. Jim Rafferty. He was a teacher at our school and he was our football coach as well. He was tall and fit and could have been a pro if he hadn't wanted to be a teacher. At least, that's what he said. I knew he was – like – in politics too. That's what my dad said, but I didn't take much notice.

'As you know, our town's on the border and things have got worse recently. The place is split between us

Catholics and the Protestants. I remember Declan trying to get through a group of loyalists on the pavement. They just walked straight at him, but when Declan stood aside a couple of our guys came along and gave him a hiding, calling my brother a coward. It was like that most of the time – it still is, some of the time.

'Anyway, I was playing in an away match against the King William school in Chapeltown. Their team was said to be brilliant, but we didn't make too much of that. We'd had a good season and Jim was pleased with us. We were making progress, he told us, progress at last, but King William was a tough nut to crack, so we weren't to rest on our laurels. Jim would never let us do that anyway – the guy was always driving us on, like we could never be good enough. But he was generous; after we won a whole load of matches he took us to McDonalds – and the burgers and shakes were on him.

'Apart from that we didn't know much about Jim, except he had a wife and four kids and lived on Balnecky Road – and that's always been a hot spot.

'Chapeltown's a small place, just like that French village you were on about. I'd been there before but not for a long time. There's this bar called O'Flannery's and a little grocery shop that sells newspapers, there are some houses and a war memorial to the Second World War in the middle of the square. There's also a big undertaker's. Cal said there'd been a lot of shootings in Chapeltown, so the undertaker must have been doing good business.

'There isn't much else in Chapeltown except the playing fields and the King William School, which is a dump; the kids have torched the place a couple of times. One of the buildings was still burnt out. The roof has collapsed and the walls are blackened with the windows boarded up. There's a big sign saying NO ENTRY – UNSAFE BUILDING and a chain fence round the ruins. It's been like that for a long time; I reckon the school and the council have run out of money.

'We lost the match by six to five, but Jim said we'd played really well and shouldn't be ashamed of ourselves. But we were. Cal was captain and he was furious with all of us, particularly me as I was one of the strikers. He told me I was rubbish. I told him to shut it and we almost had a fight, but in the end I backed off. I wouldn't take Cal on. He's tough and mean and doesn't know when to stop. Now he's out there in the dark, waiting to fix me up.

'Anyway, we were walking across the square to the bus when Jim said he'd catch us up. He wanted a pee and he'd have one in O'Flannery's bar. The bus had drawn up by the war memorial so we all got on and waited for Jim. He wasn't long coming, maybe five minutes, but he looked a bit worried. He spoke to the bus driver and what he said seemed urgent – or maybe I think it was because of what happened next.

'Just as the bus was pulling away we saw a crowd – not that many, but maybe enough to please the Orange Order band that was going to pass by on a march to Fermanagh, commemorating some British battle, or something. We could hear the distant sound of pipes and drums. I've always liked those bands, despite them belonging to the other side. I mean, they look strange in all that gear, but the tunes are stirring. I've always wanted to be in one of their bands, but of course I couldn't.

'There was a lot of stuff about the opposite side at school, and Cal was up to his neck in it. It wasn't that I didn't take the Cause seriously – I did – but there were enough problems at home, trying to make ends meet, and I was always doing newspaper rounds. It seemed like I was always on a round or at school, so the only thing to look forward to was the football. I didn't have time to think about the Cause, I told Cal, and he said, "Paddy, boy, you're traitor material. Remember that." I always did remember that.

'Anyway, a police car came roaring up, skidding to a halt in front of the bus before the driver had switched on the engine.

'One of the officers came on board and spoke to the bus driver – and then to Jim. When the officer had gone I saw that Jim was arguing with the driver again, getting even more worked up. I couldn't think why.

'The argument went on until the band was much nearer and the pipes and drums were really deafening. The band – a band dedicated to King William – had two young kids out in front, throwing batons in the air and catching them again. I got a real buzz, but I tried not to look as if I was enjoying it or Cal would be at me again.

'Then Jim suddenly stood up and said to us all, "Let's get out of the bus. We'll go up on that slope so we can take a look at the parade."

'There was a large hill just above the town and I wondered why he wanted us to scramble all the way up there when we could get a better view from the street.

'"Why don't we just drive on?" asked Cal. "Who wants to look at a band?"

'"We can't," snapped Jim, and I wondered what was biting him. Did he hate the bands as much as Cal did? Was he trying to avoid this one? "The road's blocked further up with a broken-down truck. The band's going round it, but the police say there's no access for vehicles until they're clear and we'll have to wait. So I want all you lads out of the bus and up the hill. We might as well watch the senseless pageantry while we're waiting."

'None of the team seemed to like the idea. They just wanted to get home and have their tea. But Jim insisted and we were filing out when the band began to pass us on the other side of the road, the police holding up the traffic.

'"I'd rather wait on the bus," said Cal. "They'll be gone soon."

'"Do as you're told," said Jim. "And be quick about it."

'We got off the bus and plodded reluctantly up the track to the top of the hill. Then I heard a sudden, huge crash and there was a flash of light.

'When we turned back we saw a dust cloud thickening over Chapeltown. The band weren't playing any longer and we couldn't see them either. None of us spoke or moved.

'Slowly the dust cleared but great tongues of flame lit up the sky and one of the team, I think it was Marty Robbins, said, "Holy shit!"

'"There's been a bombing," said Jim. His voice was flat, almost casual.

'The dust was clearing but all I could see was a mountain of debris. The houses and shops had disappeared. So had the war memorial. So had the police officer and his car, except that I thought I could see two wheels under a pile of rubble. One of the young kids who had been throwing up the batons was lying in the gutter.

'"There's bits of people everywhere," Cal said. He seemed surprised. Not horrified. Just surprised.

'The flames danced in the wreckage of what I thought might once have been O'Flannery's bar and suddenly I rushed forward. I had to help. There was nothing else to do but help.

'"Come back, Pat," shouted Cal.

'"Stay here!" Jim was yelling at me now, but I didn't stop.

'Slowly I began to make out that the whole square had been blasted into nothing. It must have been one hell of a big bomb. I'd seen bombings before, but not like this. And Cal had been right – there were bits of people everywhere. I saw an ear, a head with a smile on its face, a scalp of beautiful blonde hair, fingers and a torso.

'Some of the survivors were trying to pull apart the rubble and there were a lot of alarms going off, either in cars that were partly smashed or in the shops. Several mobile phones were ringing from deep in the wreckage.

'Neither Cal nor Jim nor any of the others had followed me and I stood there, not knowing what to do, almost deciding to return to the bus. Most of the band were buried under the rubble, but there was this young guy – about my age. His legs had been blown off but the rest of him was untouched. He was lying across part of a car and, do you know, there was a smile on his face, as if he were still playing his drum. I looked round for the drum, and saw it – lying untouched, like the guy's face, on the road.

'Then I heard a voice. I went over to a pile of wreckage. Smoke was pouring out, but it was slowly clearing. The voice came again. "Dad," it said. "Where are you, Dad?"

'I climbed up the pile and got as near the voice as I could. Then I called down, "Anyone there?"

'There was silence.

'"Anyone there?"

'Then a voice said, "Is that you, Dad?"

'"I'm Patrick."

'"Who are you?"

'"My name's Patrick."

'Then Jim was by my side. '"What the hell do you think you're doing? Come away. Now."

'"There's someone down there."

'"Where?"

'"A girl. Listen. Who are you?" I bawled through the wreckage.

'"I'm Katie."

'"Where are you?"

'"I don't know. There's all this stuff. I can't get my breath."

'"We'll get you out."

'"Where's my dad?"

'"I'll find him soon – but right now I'm going to start digging. Keep talking," said Jim. He was shaking all over, trying to control himself.

'I didn't feel much, except a loathing for the whole thing – like I always did. But I did realise that Jim was horrified that the bombing had done so much damage, and because he was a decent man – in a strange way he was a decent man – he had wanted to help out.

'The girl's voice had sounded very weak and I began to scrabble at the masonry. As I scrabbled, my feelings came back to me and, like Jim, I began to shake all over. I was also sweating. In fact I was sweating so much I could hardly see. I had to keep wiping the stuff off my brow. Some of the other boys had joined me and Jim was now pulling at great blocks of shattered concrete. There was the sound of sirens along the road and I knew the rescue people were coming, but we kept pulling and tearing at the debris. When I looked down at my fingernails I could see they were torn and bleeding, and yet I hadn't felt any pain.

'"Keep talking," I shouted.

'But the little girl didn't reply.

'"Are you there?" bellowed Jim.

'"Who's that?" Her voice was weaker and sounded blurred. Then she said, "It's hurting."

'"What is?"

'"I don't know. I'm hurting. Where's my dad?"

'"He's OK," said Jim without the slightest knowledge of who he was or where he might be. "Your dad's around."

'"I want him."

'"Let's dig you out first," I shouted. "Keep talking."

'But she didn't, and we began to lift the stone and concrete off more carefully because her voice had been much nearer last time, or so I thought. A man from the fire brigade came up and Jim explained what we were trying to do.

'"Can you hear me, darling?" the fire officer asked.

'The girl's voice was very weak now. "When's my dad coming to get me? I hurt. I don't like it." She made a rattling sound and the fireman called some other officers over. We all began to scrabble again.

'For the first time since I'd started trying to help the little girl I looked back. The rubble was swarming with people trying to do what we were doing – to dig and go on digging. Jim had tears streaming down his face, but Cal who had just turned up seemed unmoved.

'"Dad," came the faint cry. "I'm hurting."

'The fire brigade were hosing down the burning side of a house and some of the water was blown towards us in the strong breeze. The fine spray was refreshing and washed away some of the thick dust that had been settling over me, making my eyes sting and clogging up my lungs so that it was getting difficult to speak. Jim was rasping too as he kept calling to the little girl, promising she'd be free soon. "Hang on," he kept repeating. "Just hang on till I get to you."

'"Is that you, Dad?"

'"It surely is."

'"You haven't…got…his voice."

'"We'll soon have you out of there. You just hang on — and that's an order."

'"Go slowly now," said a woman from the fire brigade, taking off her hard hat and sitting back on her haunches. Her uniform was covered in dust and she was rasping too, her throat clogged up just like everyone else's. "Go slowly. She must be in some kind of air pocket. We don't want to bring anything else down on top of her."

'Then, suddenly, I saw a small arm, badly cut and bruised, but an arm that was moving nonetheless.

'"My name's Liz," said the fire officer. "We can see you now. What's your name?"

'Only a whisper of a voice came back. "It's Katie."

'"OK, Katie. Now this might take a bit of time. We've got to work slowly. Where are you hurting?"

'"All over."

'"Can you breathe?"

'"Yes."

'"Keep talking to us. Where do you go to school?"

'"Down the road."

'"What's the name of the school?"

'"The Heart of Our Lady." The little girl's voice was even thinner now. So she's a Catholic, I thought. Had the bombers meant to use such force? Was the bomb only meant for the band? Surely it must have been.

'"OK," said the fire officer. "We're now going to move some more of this stuff very, very carefully."

'Slowly we uncovered the little girl's face and then discovered that Katie was trapped under an iron girder. There was blood on her chest and some more oozing out of her mouth.

'"It hurts," she whispered, gazing up into Jim's face.

'"We'll have you out soon, darling. Just a few more minutes."

'But we all knew it was hopeless. She'd been crushed and releasing her would take an unbelievably long time. I glanced round for Cal and saw that he was sitting on his own a few metres away, chatting to someone on his mobile.

'"Will you stop that?" roared Jim, turning on Cal with his face twisted in rage. "Don't you have any respect?"

'Cal rang off, but didn't turn round, still sitting with his back to us. Then he said, "There's a lot of our side killed. Chapeltown's got a lot of us. That bomb was too big."

'"Shut up!" Jim yelled at him.

'Cal didn't say any more, just started punching at the keypad of his mobile. But I didn't pay much attention to that. Cal was a hard guy and I wanted to get the little girl out. I wanted to save her life – but I knew I couldn't.

'A paramedic stepped carefully over the rubble and knelt down beside Katie. He looked at her sorrowfully for what seemed an awfully long time. Then he pulled out his medical bag, drew up a syringe and injected Katie in her arm. "That'll make things easier," he said, stroking the side of her head. Katie had brown, wavy hair and her face, apart from being covered in dust, was untouched, just like the boy in the band. The paramedic shrugged at Jim. Then he took us both aside – out of Katie's hearing.

'"Can't we get her out?" Jim was very anxious.

'"The heavy lifting gear's on its way, but it's going to be too late for her."

"'How can you be so sure?" demanded Jim.

"'Her chest is crushed."

'Most of the fire brigade, including Liz, began to leave, answering other calls.

"'How many dead?" asked Jim as the paramedic zipped up his bag.

"'A hell of a lot. This is one of the biggest bombs I've seen. Why they used so much explosive I don't know."

"'To get the band?" I suggested.

"'Did they need to take out the town? Someone's made a mistake. A terrible mistake."

'The paramedic stumbled away through the rubble and we returned to where Katie was lying. Jim took her hand, feeling her pulse. "She's still alive," he whispered. "Just," he added. He began to talk to Katie reassuringly and I've never heard him be so gentle and loving. After a while Jim said softly, "Not so much in pain, my darling?"

"'Want to sleep."

"'You sleep."

"'When I wake up, will my dad come for me?"

"'And your mum too."

"'There's only him and me. No mum."

"'Then your dad will be on his way."

"'Soon?"

"'Very soon, my darling."

'Katie murmured something that I couldn't hear and again there was the awful rattling sound.

'Jim put his finger on her pulse and then her forehead. There was a pain in his voice as he said, "She's gone. Oh, Christ and Holy Mother of God, she's gone."

'I said nothing. I felt numb. What's more, I had never seen Jim in such a state. It was terrible the way she'd died. And didn't Jim have a wife and four kids of his own? One of them had to be around Katie's age.

'"They've wrecked the town centre," I said.

'"There were meant to be informers here."

'"And kids – and innocent people too."

'Cal was back, standing over me, angry and menacing. "Don't ever let me hear you speak that way again, Patrick. If I do, I'll break your legs. This is war."

'"It's a disaster," said Jim. "And if I hear *you* speak that way again, Cal, I'll break your head."

'Cal walked away with a sneer while Jim and I crouched over the body of the young girl.

'"Shall we close her eyes?" I asked.

'Gently Jim bent over her and pressed her eyelids shut. They stayed shut. I'd expected them to spring open again and fix us with that awful dead stare.

'"Where's her dad?"

'"Probably under all that rubble. I'm sorry you

had to see that."

"'I've seen dead people before. But not anyone so young." I paused and then said, "Why is Cal like he is?"

"'Because I'm like I am," said Jim quietly.

"'I don't get you."

"'You'd better not." He got up, grabbed my wrist and pulled me up beside him. He put an arm round my shoulders and squeezed me tight. "It's war. Cal's right."

"'Where are you?"

"'Right by your side." He gave a mirthless laugh.

"'You know what I mean."

'But just then the paramedic came back. "She's gone," said Jim. "You relieved the pain."

"'I'm glad to hear that."

'I turned away to see a priest giving a man the last rites. Then he crossed himself, drew his overcoat around him and walked back to the road.

"'How many dead?" I asked.

'The paramedic shrugged. "We can't be sure. With the band – there's probably over fifty. It was a big one. The worst since the Good Friday agreement."

"'You're right," said Jim.

"'Those bastards—" The paramedic was exhausted and increasingly emotional. "Why do they carry on?"

"'Some people feel there's still a war to fight." Jim's voice was almost inaudible. "I'll be getting these lads back home. I told the driver to phone ahead to say they're safe." He looked around him. "I don't think there's anything left to do here, is there?"

'The paramedic said he was sure there wasn't and Jim and I picked our way through the rubble to the bus where the rest of the boys were waiting.

'So was Cal.

'"Open your mouth and I'll shut it for you," snapped Jim as Cal started to speak.'

TEN

The Colonel was gazing into Patrick's eyes. 'Do I take that as I'm meant to take it? That your Jim was involved in the bombing? That Jim was a terrorist?'

For a moment Patrick was afraid. 'Yes,' he said after a while.

'Do *you* want some whisky?'

'I never touch the stuff.'

'Why not?'

'I'm afraid of what I might say.'

The Colonel nodded as if Patrick had just said something rather wise.

'Wasn't it out of character for Jim to put you boys at risk?'

'I think we were running late. He imagined the bus would get well clear.'

'And that's why your dad was shot? Because he put the finger on Jim?'

Patrick nodded.

'And that's why Cal's after you too?'

'I guess he knew I'd sussed Jim out. And when the police arrested Jim he reckoned I'd told my dad.'

'Where is he now?'

'I'm not sure.'

'And Cal?'

'He's out there,' said Patrick quietly.

'He won't guess where we are.' The Colonel sounded reassuring.

'The Germans flushed *you* out.'

'That was different.'

Patrick began to doze and the Colonel took another slug of whisky. There was silence between them, but Patrick found it comforting. Lying on the hard floor he felt a wall of fatigue sweep over him and suddenly he was asleep.

Patrick woke slowly, lit the candle again and checked his watch. It was two a.m. and although he'd only slept for just over an hour he was astonished to find how refreshed he felt. Even his head had stopped aching.

He glanced across at the Colonel's chair and even in the darkness he could sense he had gone. Patrick checked to make sure and then gazed up the stairs, panic surging, but the trapdoor was closed.

The whisky bottle was only a quarter full now and he had the dreadful idea that the Colonel had drunkenly decided to return to the house to 'repel boarders' – as he would have said.

Feeling shaky and apprehensive, Patrick snuffed out the candle, ran up the steps and cautiously pushed the trapdoor up, shivering in the cold air of the summer house. He moved closer to one of the windows and rubbed at the grime, but he could see nothing but the shrubbery. For a moment he was reminded of young Tom, the boy-man in the faded photograph, gazing from the window of the French church.

But Patrick could only see a dark mass of greenery, and the fear began to lock inside his stomach, giving him painful cramps. His head was hurting too and for a moment all he wanted to do was to go back to the crypt, curl up in the Colonel's empty chair and sleep.

Suddenly he remembered he'd left the trapdoor open and scurried across the floor to close it, kicking aside some of last year's leaves that had blown in through a broken window.

Then he opened the door of the summer house and slipped out into the cold night air, pushing through the overgrown shrubbery and pausing, waiting, getting a view of the darkened house under the crescent moon.

Nothing stirred.

But there was a light on in a downstairs room and Patrick guessed the Colonel had returned to the kitchen.

Had Cal and his gang gone home? Given up? Needed their beds as much as he needed his? It was possible.

Patrick wondered what to do. Should he return to

the summer house and clamber back down to the crypt? Get some more sleep? The idea was very tempting. Or should he check out the Colonel and make sure he was all right?

What would he do if he wasn't?

With a sudden shock Patrick realised he didn't want anything to happen to the old man. Weren't they both warriors in their own right? Like hell we are, he thought, with an honesty he hadn't known he possessed. He had to tell him. Had to tell the Colonel the truth.

But that would have to wait. First, Patrick had to make sure the Colonel was safe. It was the least he could do.

Slowly and cautiously, continuing to check around him, Patrick left the safety of the shrubbery and began to walk across the lawn where there was no cover of any kind. But there was long grass — almost waist high — at the back and they could be hiding there again, ready to come charging out at any moment.

Never had he felt so afraid. Every shadow seemed to be a crouching shape, full of menace. Several times he came to a halt, sure that he had seen some tiny movement in the bushes. Last time he had put the movement down to the scurryings of small animals. Then Cal and his lads had risen so menacingly, so mockingly out of the long grass.

Stopping and starting, throat dry and heart pounding, Patrick made little progress. Now he was shaking so much he could hardly walk. Then he stopped yet again. Weren't they over there, hiding in the bushes? He could almost see Cal's bulky shape. Then he realised he was looking at a pair of overgrown rusty gates that must have once been another entrance to the gardens.

He moved on and saw himself as a cat, silent as the night, padding over the wilderness lawn, ready to run at any moment, sure that danger was everywhere.

But nothing happened.

Night noises heightened the fear, touched his imagination, making him tremble. A squeal, a flutter, a rustle, a flicker, a brushing sound – he heard them all. And weren't there stealthy footsteps too?

Wanting to break into a run, instinctively forcing himself to edge along slowly, Patrick continued in fits and starts. Cold sweat was streaming down his face and he could hardly breathe, aware that he was totally exposed.

Then, to his surprise, Patrick found himself only a few steps away from the back of the house. The kitchen window was open and a cluster of crane flies, leggy, fluttering, had got in to circle round the light in their featherweight dance. Patrick shuddered. Why was he so afraid of these poor, harmless creatures, and why did his brother Declan find them so fascinating? They must be the most vulnerable things that ever flew, thought Patrick and, pressing closer to the window, he saw one of the crane flies fluttering over to a thick band of web and predictably getting stuck. You dope, thought Patrick, as he saw the insect's desperate attempts to escape the fatal stickiness.

What was it about these mindless creatures? Patrick wondered, remembering moths singeing their wings on a flame. But he'd rather encounter a moth any time. There was more substance to them.

Close to the window now, Patrick could see a spider scurrying across to attack, to paralyse and to feed on the helpless crane fly.

Hadn't he been like that? Fluttering on the edge of the web until he'd been trapped.

Declan had always known he had to keep away from Cal. He had even tried to persuade Patrick to have nothing to do with him.

Patrick had scoffed at his brother. 'Will you shut it, or will I shut you?'

But Declan, usually easy to intimidate, had taken a further risk. 'For the love of God, will you listen to me?'

'I'm making a living.'

'We don't need it.'

'I do.' Patrick punched his arm a couple of times.

His brother had turned away without retaliating – as he always did.

Now Patrick was pushing open the back door. Was the old fool really so stupid? Couldn't he secure anything – even a door? He went inside, whispering the Colonel's name.

'Who's that?' His speech was slurred. As Patrick had suspected, the old man was now blind drunk, and to his consternation the Colonel was loading a gun with trembling hands.

'For God's sake,' Patrick began. 'What are you doing?'

'I'm knitting a sweater. What do you think I'm doing?'

The gun – a shotgun – looked extremely old and Patrick felt sure it wouldn't fire. If it did, the action would probably be more fatal for the gunman than the intended victim.

'Give me that,' said Patrick impatiently.

'What does a young fool like you know about guns?'

'More than you do now, by the look of it.'

'Leave me alone.'

'You're too drunk to load that.'

'I've just loaded it.' He put the gun down on the table.

'What do you think you're up to?' Patrick was

angry now. It was as if he were the adult and the Colonel a child.

'I thought we'd be better off armed.'

'You didn't tell me you were leaving the crypt.'

'You were sound asleep.'

'I got one hell of a shock.' Suddenly Patrick was back to being the child again, deserted and abandoned.

'I'm sorry. I'd forgotten all about the shotgun. I don't know why. We'd better get back to the crypt.' The Colonel paused. 'I think your little pals have given up for the night and gone home.'

'You don't know that.'

'I sense it.'

'Well, I don't. We'll have to be careful. You should never have left the light on.'

The Colonel was aggrieved. 'How could I see to load this without a light? I could have blown my head off.'

'I'm surprised you didn't,' snarled Patrick.

The Colonel suddenly threw back his head and gave a barking laugh. 'You're not such a bad little sod, are you?'

'We must get back.'

'That's just what we're going to do.'

'And aren't you going to lock the door behind you? It *is* your house, after all.'

'Come on.' The Colonel suddenly put an arm

round his shoulder and Patrick felt a warmth, a companionship that he couldn't remember ever experiencing before.

I've got to tell him the truth, thought Patrick. I have to be honest. For once.

'Wait a minute.' Patrick paused at the open door, his elation disappearing.

'What now?'

'I thought I saw something move.'

'There's no one there.' The Colonel was just behind him and Patrick could smell the whisky on his breath. 'You're wrong. Do you understand?'

'Shut up!' hissed Patrick.

'Don't you speak to me like that.'

Patrick could feel the barrel of the shotgun poking into the small of his back. Was the drunken Colonel's finger on the trigger? If so Patrick would be shot by his own side.

'Put that bloody gun down.'

'Be quiet.'

'You could shoot me.'

'Shooting's too good for you,' snarled the Colonel, but he lowered the gun.

They stood there, waiting, Patrick staring out into the darkness.

'I'm sure I saw something move.'

'Let's get going, shall we?' The Colonel's voice was still badly slurred.

'Wait.' Patrick turned round, gazing down the long corridor. 'There's someone in the house.'

'I can't hear anything.'

'I heard…something, someone, in the sitting room.' Patrick was insistent.

The Colonel was silent.

They both listened.

The silence seemed impenetrable.

Then they both heard an object crashing to the floor.

'What's that?' The old man suddenly seemed afraid.

'Someone's kicked something over.'

They both listened again but the silence was like a wall and Patrick guessed that whoever was in the house was listening too. He grabbed the Colonel's sleeve, put a finger to his lips and pointed down the corridor, beckoning him on.

The Colonel didn't move and Patrick beckoned to him again. Slowly he led him down the corridor and they came to a halt outside the closed door of the sitting room, listening again, but hearing nothing.

Gently, Patrick began to turn the handle.

ELEVEN

They were lounging there in the darkness, occupying chairs and sofas, a couple of them sitting on the floor.

They were very still.

Then Cal stood up. 'We've come back for you, Patrick. Now why don't you just take your punishment.'

'You've broken into my house,' snarled the Colonel.

'You don't say,' said Cal, and there was laughter.

Despite the darkness of the room, Patrick recognised them all – Cal, of course, and Roy and Seamus and Ryan and Connor – and two more who must have been brought in as reinforcements – Dermot Rafferty and Felix O'Hearne. Briefly, Patrick met Dermot's accusing gaze, then looked away.

The Colonel gently pushed Patrick into the room. For a moment, he was horrified. Was the Colonel handing him over to the mob? Then the old man snapped on the light switch and, turning round, Patrick saw that he was levelling his shotgun at Cal.

Patrick turned back, seeing their pale faces, the triumph in their eyes fading.

'You're pointing a gun at me,' said Cal. His nose

was already covered in dried blood.

'You've finally woken up to what I'm doing then,' said the Colonel. 'Get out of my house or I'll shoot you.'

'You could be on a charge of murder,' commented Dermot.

Patrick knew they weren't afraid and realised the Colonel cut a ridiculous figure.

Then Felix stood up. 'Give me the gun,' he said quietly.

The Colonel turned the shotgun on him, trembling finger on the trigger.

Patrick tried to think how he could turn the situation round. The Colonel could certainly shoot someone, providing the ancient shotgun fired, but they could just as easily rush him. Patrick gazed at the steel toecaps of their boots.

'You won't be shooting me with that,' said Felix.

'I will if you come any nearer.'

Felix had his hand out now. 'Come on. Give it to me. We're not going to hurt you. We just want Patrick. Don't we, Patrick?'

'You're not taking him,' said the Colonel.

'This is nothing to do with you,' said Cal.

'Of course it is.' The Colonel's voice suddenly seemed less slurred. 'You broke into my house.'

'We came to fetch an informer.'

'Why do you call him that?'

'He betrayed someone.'

'He's a child.'

'There's a war on.' Cal spoke steadily and with great assurance.

'War? You don't know the meaning of the word.' The Colonel was contemptuous.

'I do,' said Cal, still very steadily. 'I lost my brother and a cousin to the war.'

'Give me the gun,' repeated Felix, still slowly approaching the Colonel. 'It'll be for the best if you do.'

'Keep away from me.'

Felix was now within a pace of the old man, his hand still out.

'Give me the gun.'

'No. I'll see you in hell first.' The Colonel now sounded very much in charge and seriously threatening.

'Give me the gun.' Felix came nearer. His hand was still reaching for the barrel of the shotgun.

The Colonel squeezed the trigger and fired, aiming at Felix's ankle.

The noise was not the usual dull thud of a modern weapon but a blasting sound.

Felix reeled back and Patrick could see blood oozing down his ankle, bright red, like stage blood, like it was part of a game. But this was no game.

The gang leapt to their feet and for a moment Patrick thought they were going to rush the Colonel. But he was already pointing the gun at Cal who stepped back, staring at Felix who had begun to howl like a dog. Felix leant down, gazing at his own blood on the floor, hugging his ankle and continuing to wail.

The Colonel's hands were much steadier now. 'Get out of my house and take that cowardly little bastard with you.'

'He could die from loss of blood,' said Roy, gazing at the howling Felix in disbelief.

'He won't,' said the Colonel. 'Get him out of here or I'll do the same to you.' He waved the shotgun at Cal who for once looked afraid.

'OK,' said Cal. He leant over and, in spite of his howling protests, hauled Felix to his feet. 'I'm taking him to hospital. You're going to be arrested for this.'

'I don't think so.' The Colonel was sneering now. 'I'm protecting my property and well within my rights.'

But Patrick knew he wasn't.

Struggling to carry Felix, Cal and his gang left by the broken open window of the sitting room, this time carefully avoiding the shards of glass. It was a ragged and humiliating retreat and the Colonel now seemed drunk with elation, his speech once more badly slurred.

'Good riddance,' he told Cal, who was the last to climb over the sill. 'Good riddance to filthy scum!' he bellowed.

Cal looked back. 'You've made things worse, you stupid old bastard. Much worse for you, and him.'

Cal disappeared from view, leaving Patrick with a huge sense of anticlimax. They'd be back for sure and maybe the beating would be so bad they would kill him. Patrick glanced at the Colonel who suddenly looked frail and indecisive. 'I should call the police,' he muttered.

'What good would they do?' asked Patrick bleakly. His fatigue had gone, but he was deeply afraid.

'They're paid to uphold the law.'

'But they don't – can't.'

'You consider your friend Cal outside the law.'

'Yes.'

'How absurd.' The Colonel seemed to be reflecting on something quite different, not attempting to put any meaning into what he was saying.

'What are you thinking?' asked Patrick.

'Nothing that's any of your business.'

'Do you want me to go?'

The Colonel didn't reply.

'I can easily take off now, while they're getting Felix to hospital.'

'And leave me in the lurch?'

'What do you mean by that?' Patrick was genuinely surprised.

'I shot him. That's illegal. Even if he had broken in—'

Patrick nodded.

'And then there's yourself.' The Colonel gave a hollow laugh.

'You assaulted me. Twice.' Patrick suddenly grinned at the old man. 'Don't worry. I'm not going to tell on you.'

'That wound needs stitches.'

'It'll keep. I'm safer out of hospital. Don't forget, that's where Felix's going.'

'So what do you suggest we do?' The Colonel seemed to be at a loss.

'Maybe I *should* go. I mean, what's the point of waiting? They'll only come back for me.'

'And me,' said the Colonel.

'Are you afraid?' asked Patrick curiously.

'Of a bunch of kids?' The Colonel tried to scoff, but failed badly.

'They're much more than that.'

'I'm not afraid of them,' the old man insisted. 'But they could burn my house down.'

'Then call the police.'

The Colonel hesitated. 'They can't give me

round–the–clock protection. Better to fight.'

'Fight?'

'I can handle them.' He sat down heavily on a straight-backed chair and put his shotgun over his knees. 'I'd be happy to use this again.'

'They could charge you.'

'I'm aware of that. But I'm damned if I care. I'll go down fighting.'

'Then I'll stay with you.'

'And go down fighting too? Come on, you're young and you've got a future ahead of you. You're not an old has-been like me. I don't care if I die.'

Was this the whisky talking? wondered Patrick. But he had a gut feeling the old man meant what he said.

'After all, what have I got to live for?'

'There's the next morning,' said Patrick with instinctive optimism.

'I never want to wake up to a new morning.' Rather than being self-pitying, the Colonel sounded matter-of-fact. 'I'm just whiling away my time. Waiting for the Grim Reaper, waiting for death – just like Jack did.'

'Can't we take shelter in the crypt again?' asked Patrick with sudden urgency. 'I don't think Felix needs half a dozen of them to get him to hospital. Cal may already be on his way back.'

'Could he get himself armed?' asked the Colonel in yet another sudden change of mood.

'It's possible. We'd be better off where we were.'

'Suppose they're back in the grounds already?' There was an edge of panic in the Colonel's voice.

'Maybe we should check. Let's take a look round and, if we're sure they're not on the prowl, we can make it back to the crypt. How much ammunition do you have?'

'Half a box.'

'That won't save the country.'

'It might just save us.' The Colonel seemed to be calmer and the slur in his voice was flattening out yet again.

'Let's take a look outside,' said Patrick. 'A very careful look.'

They searched the grounds for more than half an hour, the Colonel carrying his shotgun. They checked the back and then went round to the front where Patrick discovered a very different kind of wilderness.

'This was the talk of the county,' explained the Colonel in a whisper. 'I let it go when Sandra died.'

Under the light of the crescent moon, Patrick could just make out the shape of a terrace that ran down to a weed-choked lake. On either side of the terrace were sculpted heads at regular intervals, covered in moss and lichen, rising out of crumbling stone walls that were almost buried by the long rank grass.

As they scoured the ruined gardens, Patrick became more confident. There were only a few trees or bushes and, although the long grass could give Cal cover, if he so much as moved they would see him and his mob. Patrick became increasingly sure that Cal had not yet returned.

Standing by the lake, lit by wan moonlight, Patrick suddenly experienced a rush of companionship for the Colonel and once again he had the notion that they were comrades-in-arms, powerful and full of authority. Well, Cal had been sent packing, hadn't he? And Cal wasn't easy to see off.

In the middle of the lake Patrick saw a small island. In the centre stood a statue – a woman in a cloak with a sword. Then he saw the rowing boat moored up to the bank.

'Who's the statue?' he asked.

'Diana – the goddess of the moon. My wife was very fond of her so recently I took out the boat and gave her a spring clean. I haven't been on the water in years, so it was quite a treat for me – and Diana.'

'Let's row across,' said Patrick impulsively, childishly eager to get on to the island, although he wasn't quite sure why.

'We're meant to be searching for a gang of

villains – not messing about in boats.' The Colonel sounded old and tired.

'They won't be back for a while,' said Patrick confidently. 'Let's take our chance. There's no way they can get to the island. Cal's not much of a swimmer.'

'What about the others?'

'We've got the gun,' said Patrick.

'There's nothing out there.' But the Colonel's protest was weak. 'Only a statue and...' The Colonel hesitated.

'What?'

'My wife's grave.'

'You mean she's buried out there?'

'That's what she wanted.' The Colonel sounded anxious. 'I did what she wanted.'

'I think that's brilliant.' Patrick was deeply moved.

'You do?'

'Really brilliant. People should be buried where they want to be buried. Not stacked up in rows, like in a cemetery or graveyard. When did your wife die?'

'Ten years ago. Ten years of desert.'

'Let's go and take a look.' For some strange, illogical reason Patrick desperately needed to reach the island.

The Colonel smiled in the darkness but Patrick could feel his apprehension.

'All right.' The Colonel looked down at his watch.

'Just after three. That's when most people die. I call it the dying time. That's when Sandra died. Just after three a.m.'

'Can I row?' asked Patrick gently.

'If you can.'

'I've rowed before.'

'Where?'

'On the lake in the park.'

'Well, let's see what kind of oarsman you are.'

At first Patrick found himself to be an extremely incompetent oarsman, his strokes either too deep or too shallow. Several times he drenched the Colonel with a sheet of water, but the old man didn't seem to mind. Patrick could almost imagine the Colonel was his own age and that they were two boys mucking about on the lake in an old boat.

He remembered, years ago, when he and Cal had been friends, they had spent hours splashing about on the lake in the park in a hired dinghy, going round in circles and causing the attendant to shout threateningly at them over the water – but to little effect. They had been half an hour late bringing the boat back and the attendant had tried to charge them extra, but he and Cal had run away laughing as he cursed them. It seemed a lifetime ago now. As they grew up, their friendship diminished. Cal believed in the Cause. Patrick hardly even believed in himself.

'Keep her straight,' said the Colonel. 'And don't put the oars in so deep. I'm getting soaked.'

They both laughed, and after a while Patrick became more adept, soon nudging the boat into the reeds that surrounded the island. On the Colonel's instruction, he found a mooring ring on a concrete block to which he managed to attach the rope and held the boat steady while the old man struggled out. Jumping clear, Patrick followed him.

Wielding the torch, the Colonel led the way while Patrick brought up the rear with the shotgun. Eventually, round the back of the statue of Diana, the Colonel paused.

All the long grass had been cleared away from the simple tombstone, which had a vase of flowers just below the headstone.

MY BELOVED SANDRA LIES HERE
SHE GAVE ME GREAT HAPPINESS

Then there were the dates of her birth and death, carved just as simply into the stone.

Suddenly the Colonel went down on his knees and, on impulse, putting down the shotgun,

Patrick joined him.

As Patrick knelt beside the old man, he felt a sudden surge of need – the need to be honest with the Colonel at last.

'Are you praying?' he whispered.

'Just thinking.'

'Can I tell you something?'

'Of course.'

'The story I told you – about my dad, about the revenge shooting—'

'Yes?'

'It wasn't true. I made the story up.'

The Colonel said nothing and they both remained kneeling in the pale light. Patrick felt a sense of relief, as if he'd been cleansed.

'Why?' the old man asked.

'I wanted to give a good account of myself.'

'To me?'

'Why not?'

'So why are you telling me you lied? Now.'

'This is a sacred place.'

The Colonel sighed. 'Do you want to tell me the truth?'

'Yes.'

'Then go ahead.' The Colonel sat down heavily in front of the grave. Patrick joined him. 'We're just as safe here as we would be in the crypt. No one can take us unawares.'

There was a long silence. Then Patrick said, 'I've got a different story to tell – but this time it's true.'

'Let's hear it then.'

'I'm a runner. I'm given money to carry messages. It helps us out.'

'Who's us?'

'Me and my mother and brother.'

'And your father?'

'He went away years ago. My dad's in prison – and my mother's crippled. I have to look after us.'

'How did she get injured?'

'She got run over by a British armoured truck at the height of the Troubles – years ago now.'

'Is there anyone else at home?'

'My brother, Declan.'

'Is he younger?'

'By a couple of years.'

'And what kind of person is Declan?'

'Nothing like me.'

'What does that mean?'

'It means he's not some kind of sad bastard.'

'Is that how you see yourself?' asked the Colonel.

Patrick didn't reply.

'And is that why your friends are after you?'

'They're not my friends.'

'Then who are they?'

'They used to be my friends. They want to punish me.'

'What did you do?'

'They think I betrayed someone.'

'Did you, or didn't you?'

'I didn't set out to.'

'What does that mean?'

'I ran messages,' said Patrick evasively. 'The results are sometimes obvious.'

'Did you get paid?'

'Yes.'

'What did you spend the money on?'

'I got a new washing machine for Mum – and a TV for Declan's room.'

'And yourself?'

'Nothing much.'

'You didn't want anything?'

'I wanted *them* to have stuff. Declan and Mum.'

'Do you want to tell me what you really did?'

'Yes. Yes I do.'

TWELVE

'I knew Jim, our football coach, better than most of the other players because his son Dermot was a mate of mine. He was another member of the team, but Jim didn't do his son any favours. Dermot had to earn his place just like anybody else. Just like me. But we played another game – much more scary than football.

'I used to spend a lot of time at Jim's home because Dermot had a computer and I didn't. Dermot was always willing to share.

'A few months before the bombing, Jim suggested we both ran some messages for him – and if we kept our mouths shut and remembered what to do, we'd be well paid.

'We ran coded messages that had to be memorised. I can't tell you who we ran the messages to, but I soon guessed they were coded signals that would activate either sleepers – agents who had been in place for a long time but had not yet been called on – or terrorist cells that were ready for immediate action.

'"The telephones are tapped at home," Jim told us. "And most of us are under surveillance. But no one's going to suspect a couple of kids running errands. Not for a while anyway."

'Dermot and I were active for two months during the period that covered the Chapeltown bombing.

'We were well paid. Dermot bought himself a mountain bike, officially a present from his dad. I gave my earnings to my mother. I think she guessed where they were coming from and she was very uneasy at first. But eventually she went out and bought the new washing machine. I felt good about that. Later we managed to get the TV for Declan. But it worried him and he hardly ever watched the thing.

'"We've got our secret language," he told me. "But it's not strong enough, is it? You're already fluttering in the web – and they'll never let you fly away." It looks as if he was right, doesn't it?'

For once the Colonel was silent, and Patrick continued.

'When I looked in the papers and saw the shootings and the bombings I knew what had set them in motion. But the money was more important. I love my mother. I wanted her to have her few little extras. And Declan. God knows, they'd never had much before. I refused to see how upset they were getting, how badly I was bringing us all down.

'But the Chapeltown bombing changed all that. And then it got worse. I'd been in trouble at school, not having done my history homework for a new teacher called Gerry Mills. He was quite a young guy,

144

but he was still hard on us – much harder than most other teachers.

'One afternoon I was the only kid in the detention room. I knew plenty of others who hadn't done their homework, so I wondered resentfully why I was being singled out. I discovered why when Gerry Mills came and stood by my desk.

'"I hear you're a likely lad who likes to earn a bob or two."

'"I don't know what you mean." I immediately began to panic. What did he know? How did he know? And who was he?

'"Let's just get one thing straight, Patrick."

'"What's that, sir?"

'"If you try and stitch me up I'll deny everything. It'll be your word against mine. Do you understand?"

'I shrugged.

'"Now I'm an anxious man, Patrick – and do you know why I'm an anxious man?"

'"No, sir."

'"I want to get rid of a bob or two. Maybe more. Maybe more like five hundred pounds."

'"Five hundred?" I was gaping at him now.

'"I gather you and your mother would find that kind of money useful."

'"Anyone would."

'"I could even run to seven."

"'Hundred?'"

"'You bet. Or even a grand.'"

"'You're winding me up.'"

"'I'm not.'"

"'I don't believe you.'" And at that stage I certainly didn't.

"'How about five hundred now – and five hundred on delivery?'"

"'Delivery of what?'"

"'I hear you've been running some errands.'"

'Immediately, I was even more afraid. "Are you a teacher, or what?" I asked him.

"'We won't go into that.'"

"'You an undercover cop?'"

"'Nothing so exciting. Now do you want the money or don't you?'"

'I didn't reply.

"'Well, maybe your mother could use it.'"

'I still didn't reply and he gazed at me steadily. There was a long silence between us.

"'Who are you working for?'" I asked him.

'But he didn't reply. Instead, he said, "Just in case you're thinking of grassing me up – remember your mum. Remember how precious she is to you."

'A wave of ice-cold anxiety surged through me. "What about my mother?"

"'You love her, don't you?'"

'"Yes."

'"You wouldn't like anyone to hurt her."

'"For Christ's sake—"

'"All right, Patrick. If I can trust you, no one's going to hurt her."

'"She's crippled."

'"I know that."

'"How do you know so much about me?"

'"It's my business to know things."

'I felt a surge of raw panic. What was I getting into? What was I being forced into? For I knew I had no choice. Mills seemed to have too much on me.

'Gerry Mills was a good-looking man, with dark hair and a handsome face. He wore his teachers' "uniform" of grey slacks, brogues, sports jacket and a neatly knotted tie. He was a good teacher, but now I guessed he was something else too, and although he seemed so ordinary, here he was, threatening to hurt my mother.

'"What do you want me to do?" I asked him.

'"I want the name of the man you're running for."

'"I don't know the name."

'"I don't believe you." He was smiling and tapping a pencil on the desk. The smile was getting fixed.

'"It's true. The running's done through someone else."

'"And who is that someone else?"

"'A boy. A kid my age."

"'He's here – in the school?"

"'No. He goes to St Edmunds."

"'His name?"

"'I only know him as Mickey."

"'Mickey who?"

"'I don't know his other name."

"'Can you describe him?"

'I remember stuttering as I hurriedly made up the description. "He's smaller than me."

"'Younger?"

"'I told you, he's the same age."

"'Describe him."

"'He's short and dark with a…a small purple patch on his forehead."

"'A birthmark?"

"'Or maybe a burn."

"'Sounds more like a birthmark to me. Go on."

"'He's small and dark—"

"'So you said. What's his name again?"

'For a terrible moment, I couldn't remember my own invention. The hesitation seemed to give me away completely. "Mickey," I said lamely. There was another long silence.

"'I don't believe your Mickey exists. I think it's you who's taking the Mickey, Patrick."

"'That's not true, I tell you."

'There was a knock on the door and Mills said, "Get on with your work."

'He looked across at the door and so did I as the Head came in. "Only one?" he asked.

'"They're getting the message and handing in homework on time."

'"Well, I'm off. I'll leave you to it." The Head hurried away.

'There was another long silence.

'"Come clean, Patrick. It'll be easier for your mum if you do."

'I began to sweat. "I'll call the police," I said wildly.

'Mills laughed. "Go ahead."

'"Who are you?"

'"Your history teacher. Remember?"

'"You're more than that. You are the police, aren't you? Or someone bloody near them."

'"Come on, Patrick. Let's get it over with."

'I was silent and Gerry Mills looked at his watch. I noticed it had a complicated dial. Was it a divers' watch? Or a James Bond watch that spat bullets with an ability to stun at forty metres? Then I regained my sense of reality.

'"Someone will call on your mother."

'"No!"

'"Then tell me."

'"OK. It's...his name is...Jim Rafferty."

'Mills nodded. "He's on the staff here."

'"Yes."

'"You're not making that up?"

'"I'd be a fool if I did."

'"I don't think you're a fool, Patrick. I think you're a promising lad."

'"Who are you?"

'"Your history teacher," he repeated.

'"What's going to happen?" But by this stage I was numb and couldn't really care less what was going to happen.

'"Tell me how you operate."

'"I deliver messages. They're made up of numbers."

'"And who do you deliver them to?"

'I told him and after what seemed like an eternity the detention was over.

'"You can be on your way now, Patrick," he told me as I gathered up my bag.

'"Suppose Jim finds out I grassed him?"

'"He won't."

'"What are you going to do about him?"

'"It's not down to me."

'When I got home, Mum was in her wheelchair, cooking the supper. She was frying spam.

'"Patrick. I want to talk to you."

'I sat down, exhausted. Was this to be another interrogation?

'"I want to talk about the money."

'It *was* to be another interrogation.

'"I might give it up," I said.

'"I don't want you to go on earning money that way."

'"It's hard for you to manage."

'"Yes—"

'"I'm up for a last payment."

'"Has something happened?" She looked very anxious.

'"No."

'"You look different."

'"Different in what way?"

'"Scorched."

'"That's a weird thing to say."

'"I can see it in your eyes. Give it up, Patrick. I don't want the money."

'"We'd be back to the handouts."

'"I'd rather have the handouts. I want to keep our noses clean. You know what I feel about it all."

'"OK."

'"You'll give up the running?" She looked cautiously pleased.

'"It's not as simple as that—"

'"There's something you're not telling me." The

pleasure was over and the alarm was back.

'I leant over her wheelchair and kissed her. "I love you."

'"Do you think they'll let you go?"

'"I'll tell them I reckon I'm being watched."

'"This country," she said. "It's getting like a communist state. Everybody's spying on everybody else."

'The next day I spoke to Dermot. "You'll have to tell your dad I'll not be running for him again."

'"Why?" Dermot looked at me with suspicious hostility. "Who's changed your mind?"

'"Nobody. I just don't want to do it any longer."

'"Someone's been at you."

'"It's on my conscience."

'"Bollocks. You need the money."

'"Mum can do without it."

'"Yes?" He was laughing at me, but in a dangerous way. "I tell you, Patrick – you'll go on running for us till my dad stops needing you."

'"I tell you – I just don't want to go on with it."

'"What the hell does that mean?" Dermot looked at me closely. "There's something, isn't there?"

'Was it so obvious? First my mother and now Dermot. I thought I might as well have a sign on my back saying FINGERED.

'"There's nothing," I said.

'"There's something." Dermot was insistent.

'"It was the bombing. I was there. You weren't."

'"You've seen bombings before."

'"Not as big as that one."

'"It was an accident."

'"What?"

'"There was some kind of mess-up over the explosives."

'"How can you mess up explosives? Anyway, I want out. I'll tell your dad to his face if you like."

'"There's no need."

'"Why?"

'"I'll tell him."

'I wondered what Dermot was going to say and the more I thought about it, the more worried I got.

'I had good reason to be worried. Cal stopped me on the way home from school. He was looking sad – and when Cal looks sad he's mean.

'"I want you."

'Dermot was with him. That meant worse trouble.

'"I haven't got time."

'Dermot took my arm. "You've got all the time in the world," he said gently. Then his grip tightened.

●

'They took me up an alley into the bombed-out remains of an old dance hall. In the foyer there were hundreds of paper cups lying on the floor, tumbled from split-open packets, and a tattered poster saying IT TAKES TWO TO TANGO. I saw a dried pile of vomit near the old box-office window and some broken glass.

'Dermot picked up a sliver of the glass and held it to my face.

'"Tell us," said Cal. "Tell us what's going on."

'"I'm sick to my gut."

'"What with?"

'"The bombing. That kid. The—"

'"Shut up!" said Dermot. "Shut the fuck up." The sliver of glass came nearer to my mouth. Would he gash my lips? If he did they'd never heal. I'd have a twisted mouth. The idea of him cutting my lips terrified me. I'd tell them anything providing they didn't cut my lips.

'"Who approached you?" asked Cal.

'"OK," I said. "OK. I don't know who he really is – but he's going under the name of Mills. Gerry Mills." I realised I was getting in too deep – so deep that I could be in real danger.

'"The history teacher." Dermot gave a whistle. "I don't believe it."

'"Nice one," said Cal.

154

'"What did you tell him?" asked Dermot.

'"Nothing."

'"What did he want to know?"

'"Who I was running for."

'"If you told him, you're a dead man." Dermot still had the broken glass perilously close to my lips.

'"I'm not a grass," I said, praying I sounded convincing.

'"How much pressure did Mills put on you?"

'Again I had to invent. Why was I suddenly so bad at inventing? "He said I'd get arrested."

'"What for?" asked Dermot.

'"In connection with the Chapeltown bombing."

'"You're sure he didn't mention your mum?" asked Cal viciously. "Your poor old crippled mum?"

'"No."

'"I believe he did," said Cal. "And if he did, you *would* have told him everything."

'"I didn't tell on anyone."

'"Does Mills want to see you again?"

'"Yes."

'"Well – he's got you on the spot, hasn't he?" said Dermot.

'They were both so confident. They were both so right. But no one cared about my predicament. They might never have been my friends.

'Dermot moved the sliver of broken glass up a

bit until it was against my cheek. Then he dug the glass in and I could feel my flesh tear and the warm flow of blood.

'"That'll just be a warning," said Dermot, putting down the glass.

'"We'll need to assess the situation." Cal was already walking away. "If it's bad, you're a dead man."

'I lay in bed wide awake, unable to sleep, listening to the chatter of the TV. I imagined Mum sitting downstairs, watching the news. She could get herself out of the wheelchair and into bed or on to the toilet by a series of winches and pulleys. I'd got so used to seeing her like that I couldn't remember the time when I hadn't. Yet it was only a few years ago that she'd been run over by the army.

'My grandmother looked after me while Mum was in hospital. When she finally came out, Mum could barely cope and I learnt to do everything for her – as if she were a child that it was my responsibility to look after. I did it all myself – I wouldn't let Declan help at all.

'Later, as the house was fixed up with better equipment, she could do most things for herself. But sometimes the equipment broke down and I had to look after her again. She was just as embarrassed as she had been before – but I wasn't. I loved taking care of her and I'd always reckoned that if anyone hurt her, so much as threatened her, I would have killed them.

'Now the threat was real.

'Mother of God, whatever was I going to do?

'I lay there all night, thinking about them hurting her and then, in the early dawn, I fell into a light sleep, dreaming about Dermot stealing in through the back with his sliver of broken glass and Mills knocking at the front door with a switchblade in his pocket.

'I woke, drained and exhausted, and forced myself to get up for school, to face my mother over the breakfast table when I was at my weakest.

'"What was happening last night?" she asked as she cooked the egg and bacon and fried bread that she always gave me and Declan – and that day made me feel profoundly sick.

'"I was asleep. Like as usual."

'"You must have been having terrible nightmares."

'"What makes you think so?"

'"You kept calling my name – and telling them to stop."

'"Telling who? To stop what?"

'"I don't know. I think I was being attacked. What's going on, Patrick?"

'"If anyone else asks me that—"

'"So there *is* something."

'"There's nothing. I can guarantee that."

'"Can you really?"

'"Yes. Mum – I can't eat all this today. I'll just have some toast."

'All this time, Declan was quiet, head down over his plate.

'"But I've done your usual."

'"I don't want my usual."

'"There must be something wrong then."

'"This is one day I'd like a change."

'Suddenly I couldn't stand it any longer and I stood up, grabbing some toast and running for the door. "I've got to go to school early today."

'"Why? You're usually late—"

'Usually this, usually that. I bit back what I was going to say. It would hurt her – but not as much as glass and knives.

'"I've got to play football."

'"At this time?"

'"There's a new team being chosen."

'My mother looked at me as if I were crazy. "But you haven't got your kit."

'"I don't need my kit."

'"But—"

'"This is dribbling practice. I don't need my kit." The lie was obvious and Declan kept glancing at me and looking away.

'"Look, Patrick, I know there's—"

'Something wrong, I thought. Something wrong. Something wrong. The words beat to a drum-like rhythm in my head and didn't stop until I was out on the road, clogged with traffic as usual, running as hard as I could for the sheer sake of running.

'Someone shot him as he crossed the playground, just before break began. Later, Dermot told me that a masked gunman had ridden up on a motorbike, fired through the railings and then ridden away again. There was a neatness to the attack. A couple of holes in the middle of his chest. The gun must have had a silencer because his body wasn't discovered until break.

'As the crowd gathered, I pushed my way through. Gerry Mills, history teacher and something else, lay on his back in a lake of blood, eyes fixed on the steel-grey sky.

'Without realising what I was doing, I knelt down beside him, anxious to know if he was dead. I hoped so. I prayed so. I still went to Mass each Sunday, but here I was, wishing a man dead.

'But he wasn't. His mouth opened and there was a mumbling, but I couldn't make it out and hoped no one else could either. Then he choked and a spume of blood like a fountain flew high in the air and splattered down, covering his chest. Gerry Mills twitched. In his hand was a packet of sandwiches that had broken open. A pigeon flew down and grabbed a crust.

'The crowd moved back a little.

'But no teachers had come.

'I felt a strange sense of grief as Mills lay there, still twitching, with a big, bold pigeon pecking at his sandwich.

'Someone clapped their hands to drive the pigeon away, but others appeared and there was more clapping, as if Gerry Mills's death was being applauded.

'Then one of the other teachers, Mrs Ryan, pushed through the crowd and gave a shrill cry.

'But my momentary grief had faded. I joined in the clapping to keep the pigeons away, but really I *was* applauding. Mills was dead. And maybe I was safe.

'Then I saw Cal, at the front of the crowd.

'How long had he been there? Had I just missed seeing him? We exchanged glances. Foolishly, I grinned. He didn't.

'Later that afternoon we were assembled in the school hall that smelt of polish and sweat, and sitting on the floor we listened to what the Head had to say.

'Mr Dewer was tall and pale with a fussy little beard and a bald head. I had never thought much of him, but this afternoon was different. He spoke so movingly that I had to fight back the tears.

'"I wanted you to know that Gerry Mills, although on the staff here for only one short term, had proved himself a caring teacher. To have him gunned down in our playground is a terrible thing – but much worse for his wife and small children. Gerry Mills was a church-going man and, as you know, he made extra time for our special needs groups. A good man. A caring man."

'I glanced at Jim, sitting at the side of the hall. He was looking down, hands clasped round his knees.

'"In these troubled times, we all need to say our prayers – publicly and privately – and now in particular for Gerry Mills's wife, Veronica, and their two children, Stephen and Erin."

'Father Joseph then got up from his chair. He began to pray and my gaze returned to Jim who was now standing, as we all were. He looked sombre.

'"We commend our brother to the forgiveness of God our Father and pray that as he has been united with Christ in death he may also share in his resurrection to eternal joy."

'I still watched Jim – in fact, I couldn't take my eyes off him. He was much more relaxed now as he stood head and shoulders above the other teachers, his face composed, head bowed and arms by his sides.

'Then one of the Heads of Year got up and told us

that there would be no school next day. I had a feeling of guilty pleasure and thought I'd go fishing and think about what had happened.

'As we filed out, the corridors seemed full of police officers and the place on the playground where Gerry Mills had lain dying was surrounded by police tape. A caravan, the police incident room, was parked a few metres away. Soon a long queue built up as we were each questioned by a police officer. I spoke to a woman who had a list on a clipboard and I could see from a quick glance at the names that she was questioning class after class.

'"Your name is Patrick O'Leary?" she asked.

'"Yes."

'"Of nineteen Tullamore Street?"

'"That's right."

'"Did you see Mr Mills before he was shot this morning?"

'"No."

'"Does he teach you?"

'"Yes – on a Tuesday and Thursday morning."

'"Did he seem in any way agitated?"

'"This isn't a Tuesday or Thursday morning, miss." I hadn't meant to embarrass her. She must have questioned so many pupils that she was beginning to make mistakes. I didn't feel afraid of her. In fact I felt quite sure of myself.

"'I'm sorry." She flushed slightly. "Did you see him at all – in the corridors – or in the playground?"

"'No."

"'So your last lesson with Mr Mills would have been on Tuesday morning?"

'Today was Wednesday and knowing she was still embarrassed I tried to help her. "Yes, and he was the same as usual."

"'What does that mean – the same as usual?"

"'He was a good teacher. He always made the lessons interesting."

"'He was new to the school?"

"'Started this term."

"'And you liked him?"

"'Yes. We all did." Somehow I felt anxious to establish that Mills had a good reputation and there was a neat and tidy ending to his life. Why, I don't know, particularly after the threats he'd made. But I think I was still in shock. We were all in shock. Your history teacher doesn't get gunned down every day, not in your own school playground. And somewhere, refusing to go away, was the knowledge that he'd been gunned down because of me.

"'He didn't seem in the least distracted?"

"'No."

"'Or anxious and watchful?"

"'Not at all."

"'What about the school grapevine? Did you hear anything about Mr Mills?"

'I shook my head, and then added, "No, nothing at all." I must seem so negative, I thought, and guessed that was what we'd all sounded like – whether we knew anything or not.

"'Thank you, Patrick." The police officer turned to the next in line and I headed for the school gates, pausing to look at the place where Gerry Mills had spouted blood.

'When I got home, Declan was up in his room as usual, but Mum was hysterical. She gathered me into her arms while I knelt by her wheelchair and burst into tears. I held her hard and tried to soothe her.

"'No one was around," I said. "The playground was empty. The gunman shot him a few minutes before break. He must have had a free period and—"

"'A few minutes? My God, he could have shot hundreds of you."

"'He had his sights on Mr Mills."

"'And what have you been mixed up in? Keeping company with that Cal."

"'I don't keep company with him."

"'You always have done."

"'I don't now."

"'He's mixed up in all this – just like his dad. Cal's

164

a menace. Better to keep clear of him. You shouldn't even be playing on the same team."

"'Playing football doesn't make him a friend." It certainly didn't.

'Gerry Mills's death was on the early evening news. It was strange seeing the blurred photograph. He could have been anyone. "His death is being regarded as another sectarian shooting." I thought the reporter looked bored. There'd been so many shootings. They were routine.

"'So none of you'll be going to school tomorrow? Why give you a day off? Some will be relishing that," said my mother.

"'The police will be checking the place out."

"'As well they might. What with that terrible bombing and now this, we're in the thick of it all right." She went on, half-grumbling at me and half-grumbling to herself, until there was a knock on the door. Just one knock.

'She was clearly terrified, but I felt numb. Too much had happened; I couldn't take anything else in.

'The knock came again.

'The numbness went away and I felt the same fear as my mother. Your sergeant – Jack – he didn't understand that his appointment with death couldn't be put off. But I did.

'"Don't open the door," Mum advised. She was shaking.

'"I've got to."

'"You don't have to do anything you don't want." Her voice was crisp and I realised that my mother was suddenly taking over at last, helping me to make some kind of plan. I was grateful to her.

'The knock came again. This time twice and full of authority.

'"I'd better go," I said. "If they go on knocking, Declan could take it into his head to come down."

'With some dexterity, Mum turned her wheelchair and started to head for the door.

'"Don't be stupid," I hissed at her.

'"I'll go," she said.

'"No chance of that." I pulled at her chair, but she had locked the brakes.

'"Let me go, Patrick. They won't harm me."

'"How do you know that?"

'"I'm going to open the door," she insisted. "If there's anything wrong, you can cut out round the back."

'"If there *is* something wrong they'll have covered the back. That's pretty obvious, isn't it?" But the fear was creeping inside me, gnawing away, and all my reason was going. Maybe she *should* open the door.

'"I'll tell you what," Mum said.

'"What?"

'"Get out the toilet window. A skinny boy like you should be able to squeeze through. You can cut over the road and into Mrs Lewis's garden. Then you can make your way over the fences."

'I looked at her incredulously. I couldn't believe my mother was giving orders like she was an officer in the army. Mum's recognition that the situation was critical made me feel even more afraid.

'Then Mum unlocked the brakes of her wheelchair and steered herself through the door to the hall and up to the front door. The low-level lock had been put on a few months ago so that she could open up when Declan and I weren't there.

'Some instinct for self-preservation made me run into the toilet and lock the door.

'I listened and could just hear them talking.

'"What do you want?" Mum asked.

'"We'd like to talk to Patrick," said Cal.

'"There's an awful lot of you needing to talk to Patrick." She sounded very bitter. "None of you are welcome in my house. Now go away."

'"We can't do that," said Cal. "We've come for Patrick."

'"What do you want with him?"

'"He's grassed up Jim Rafferty. Jim's been arrested for the Chapeltown bombing. Of course, he had nothing to do with it."

'I heard Connor's giggle, high-pitched and out of control.

'"Patrick would never get Jim Rafferty into trouble. So beat it – before I call the police."

'"We need to see him." Cal wasn't going away.

'Would they hurt her – just as Gerry Mills had threatened?

'"Either let us in or we'll have to push you out of the way," said Connor, giving his high-pitched laugh again.

'Then I heard Mum yelling fit to bust and I almost went out to her. She kept on yelling and I heard Declan's feet coming down the stairs. Tears streamed down my face at the thought of what could happen to them. Even so, I opened the window, stood on the toilet seat and squeezed out, dropping to the ground, scrambling to my feet, racing across the road and beginning to vault over the garden fences. It was only when I was on the second fence that the lavatory window opened again and I heard Connor shouting.

'They were on to me and I knew they wouldn't give up.' Patrick turned to the Colonel and half-sobbed, 'I hope they didn't hurt them.'

'That's unlikely,' the Colonel replied calmly. 'It's the women who are the strong ones in this country. They wouldn't dare lay a finger on her.'

But Patrick noticed that the Colonel hadn't mentioned Declan.

'You've been very honest,' said the Colonel. His gun was lying across his knees.

'I'm not proud of what I did,' Patrick mumbled. 'I put my mother's life in danger – not to mention Declan's.'

'So Jim was arrested?'

'The information I gave Mills must have got back pretty fast.'

'And Jim had no chance of running. Like yourself.'

'He can't run with a family.'

'Not so easily,' admitted the Colonel.

'And, wherever he went, they'd get him. Eventually. So it's a good thing they got him now.'

The Colonel nodded. 'And you ran to me.'

'Much good that did me.' Patrick laughed angrily.

'We can fend them off.'

'For a while.'

'So you reckon you might as well give yourself up.' The Colonel paused. 'What'll they do to you?'

'They'll give me a beating.'

'Is that all?'

'You don't know what their beatings are like. Those boots – with steel toe caps. I can—'

'You're an informer,' stated the Colonel.

'I'd never have taken his money. He threatened my mum.'

'There's no reason to believe your story – although I *do* believe you.'

'Why?'

'You didn't have to tell me all this.'

'Maybe not,' said Patrick. 'But you were straight with me – so I should be straight with you.'

'Yes,' said the Colonel. There was a long silence between them. 'You've been straight—'

Patrick looked up at the old man curiously. 'You were straight?'

'No,' said the Colonel. 'I was lying. Just like you.'

THIRTEEN

Patrick gazed at the Colonel in amazement. Although he'd had some doubts about the Colonel's story, he'd never thought the old man would admit to lying.

'Why did you lie?'

'I've always lied. Because I was afraid — at first. Later, because I wanted my wife to go on respecting me, loving me. There are many more "becauses". Now, do you want to hear the truth?'

Patrick nodded.

'Row me to the bank. They won't stay away for ever. We've got to get back to the crypt. We're too exposed here.'

'You've got your gun.' Patrick wanted a grown-up to take over. A grown-up with a gun.

'They'll bring back weapons — and I don't have much ammunition left. An old soldier knows when to beat a strategic retreat.'

Patrick looked at his watch. It was just before four a.m. and there was a grey band of light in the sky.

'Dawn,' muttered the Colonel, getting up stiffly. 'We're running out of time.'

•

Patrick rowed over the lake as quietly as he could and, when they reached the bank, he tied the boat to the mooring post and helped the Colonel out.

The old man had become very stiff, sitting on the island, and as he tried to disembark he stumbled and would have fallen into the water if Patrick hadn't grabbed his arm, sending the antique shotgun overboard. It sank immediately. The Colonel swore. Patrick stood swearing too, feeling awful inside, inadequate and stupid, and now of course, defenceless.

'Come on.' The old man grabbed his hand and began hauling him along as if he were some frightened child, but Patrick didn't try to wrench his hand away. To his surprise he realised he needed the comfort.

They stole across the wilderness lawns, the old man wheezing and Patrick gazing nervously into the foliage. Surely to God, Cal would have returned by now. What was keeping him? He couldn't have been frightened off. Not Cal.

But they made the shrubbery in safety and then the summer house, and were soon clambering down the ladder. As Patrick closed the trapdoor, he and the Colonel were plunged back into the earthy womb-like darkness.

For a while they were silent.

Then Patrick said, 'Shall I light a candle?'

'Let's save it.' He could hear the Colonel slurping

whisky. First of all he'd been a drunken old man with a gun. Now he was a drunken old man without a gun.

'You going to tell me your story then?' asked Patrick. 'The real story.' He felt better now, shut away in their hiding place.

'It's all a bit – painful.' The Colonel sounded lame.

'So was mine,' said Patrick.

'I've tried so hard to bury the truth; it's almost been overlaid by the story I made up. After all, I've been telling it for over sixty years.'

'To everyone?'

'To as many as would listen.'

'You must have got the details right then.'

'It was an alibi. You'd know all about that.'

The Colonel took another swig from the whisky bottle and Patrick began to get anxious. 'Do you think you should drink any more? You might get confused. Cal might come.'

'There's not much left,' said the Colonel, almost pleading. 'I might as well finish it off.'

'Did you tell your wife the truth?'

'God bless her, no. Not a word of it.'

'Couldn't you confide in her?'

'I've never felt like confiding in anyone. Not till you turned up.'

'And why me?'

'Because time is running out.'

'What's that meant to mean?'

'I'm going to die.'

'You know that for sure?'

'Nothing is for sure – except death.'

'I think you're pissed.'

'And you'd be right. Now – do you want to hear the truth or not? We may not have much time.'

'So tell me.'

'Forget Jack. Forget Field Security. Forget my heroism. Just remember the French family. The Dupois family.'

'I don't get you.'

'You will. I changed the names to protect the innocent, as the old movies used to say.'

'What *is* the truth?'

'There was just a couple of us. Me and Private Tom Bruce. We were on our own.'

'In the crypt?'

'For a while, and then in Monsieur Dupois's cellar.'

The Colonel laughed loudly, but there was no humour in the sound.

'For God's sake,' said Patrick. 'Don't make so much noise.'

With some difficulty, the Colonel got up and lit the candle. Then he staggered back to his chair and sat down again.

'I thought you wanted to save the candle,' said Patrick.

'Changed my mind.' The Colonel looked jaundiced in the tepid light and terribly, terribly old. Patrick thought he would reach for the whisky bottle again, but he didn't. 'What was that?' he whispered suddenly, gazing up at the trapdoor.

'I didn't hear anything.'

'Will you let me get on uninterrupted then?'

'I'm not stopping you.'

'OK. Well, forget the cast of thousands. Think of the two of us – me and Private Tom Bruce. Think of safety, sanctuary. Think of cellars and crypts and islands. All places of safety where we can hide from the enemy.' He paused. 'There was this man, Francois Armand, he was in what would soon be the Maquis – the French resistance. Later on they became a force to be reckoned with, knocking out installations – railways, communications, German transport – and the like.

'When the French surrendered, the British forces had to retreat and I found myself leading a small platoon of survivors back to the Normandy beaches, going undercover during the day and travelling by night.

'While we were hiding out in the crypt of a church, Armand came to see me. The number of men in the platoon was rather higher than I told you – over forty in fact, although most of them were walking wounded - but Armand said that my men could be hidden in twos and threes in surrounding villages and would be well looked after. If we were prepared to do them a favour. And it certainly was a favour. They wanted our guns and ammunition – because they were in short supply themselves.

'The Maquis had an objective – ambushing a train loaded with German troops. They had managed to damage a bridge, using their own landmines, but they hadn't put it completely out of action. Still, they reckoned the troop train would slow down to about five miles an hour for the damaged bridge, and just before that there was a cutting, which was apparently very narrow, very high, almost like a ravine. So an awful lot of Germans could be killed by a few Frenchmen if they had enough arms – which they hadn't unless we gave them ours.

'Naturally I asked if we could join them, but Armand said we weren't in good enough shape, and he was right. I weighed up the odds and decided that with a few days' rest the men could revive sufficiently to make the last push to the beaches. The French could well provide basic medical aid too. Of course it meant leaving us unarmed, but even if we were cornered, the guns and ammunition we had wouldn't hold the Germans off for long.

'I consulted with my sergeant and we both agreed we should back up the French and get a secure rest-up in return. Armand then explained exactly how the platoon would be split up and where my men would be hidden. I memorised the locations so that I could bring them all together again in a few days' time.

'Tom and I were given Monsieur Dupois and his family. We were well fed and the Germans didn't come looking for us. The ambush of the train was due to be carried out in a week but we would have to move on long before that in case the evacuation finished and we were stranded on the coast. In the meantime we seemed reasonably safe in the Dupois cellar.

'Except that I made a mistake – a very big mistake. I suddenly realised I'd left my army knife back in the crypt of the church – it would be a pretty good give-away if any German patrol turned up to check the church out.

'I told Tom how careless I'd been and how I'd go out and retrieve the knife. Tom disagreed. He reckoned it would be much better if one of the family went over to the church for the knife; just because the German patrols hadn't been around didn't mean they might not suddenly turn up. The overall plan to try to make the beaches dressed in those damned boiler suits was still on, and I told Tom that as I wouldn't be padding around in British army uniform no one was going to look at me twice. I was a fool. An arrogant fool.'

'So the Germans did come?' asked Patrick.

'No,' said the Colonel. 'They didn't. I went to the crypt, got the knife and returned to the cellar – all without a German patrol appearing in the vicinity. So the obvious didn't happen. But the next afternoon a German patrol *did* arrive; apparently I'd been seen by someone who wanted to make some money. I must have looked wrong.'

Patrick interrupted. 'They were like me. An informer.'

'I'll be the judge of that,' said the Colonel briskly. 'Now don't interrupt. We don't have the time for that.

'Tom had been right – I was a fool to go out, but I'd been feeling incredibly claustrophobic in the cellar. We'd been there a few days and Tom was getting on my nerves – as he often did. So my brief excursion was to get a breath of fresh air as much as to get my knife. Either way, I took a risk that was incredibly stupid.'

'The crypt couldn't have been much of an improvement on the Dupois's cellar,' Patrick observed.

'You're interrupting again,' snapped the Colonel. 'Aren't you interested?'

'Of course I am. I just thought—'

'If you let me continue, I'll tell you what happened.' The Colonel cleared his throat. 'That

178

afternoon, at about three, there was a knock on the door of the cellar. It was Henri Dupois. He told me there was a German patrol up the road, systematically searching the houses. I could see he wanted Tom and me to leave before they got any nearer, so we crept out through the kitchen garden and set off, keeping to the fields, moving cross-country, trying not to be spotted, hoping we'd be able to join our regiment on the beaches. Perhaps they were all making the same trip – having been warned by the French or having got sick of waiting for me to contact them. I felt very responsible for what had happened – well, obviously I did, but at least we'd got away and the other members of the platoon were in other villages. Tom was very loyal; he didn't even hint at how stupid I'd been and I was grateful for that.

'I thought we were going to get away with it. That night we slept in a ditch and the next morning we got up early and headed for Dunkirk. At least we felt reasonably fit again and we were making good progress until lunchtime when we were climbing a ridge – and saw a German patrol in the valley.

'We saw them. They saw us.

'We ran for it, but they must have called up another patrol. I remember doubling back through thick undergrowth. I felt like you must have felt, Patrick. There didn't seem to be anyone around, but

I sensed them stalking us, waiting to close in.

'We came to a copse and paused for a moment. There was a deep silence, as if we were in a padded room. I think we knew we'd walked into a trap, but we still couldn't detect any movement. Then there was a shot. A single shot like a single knock and Tom gasped. He was still standing there, but with a hole in his head. Then all the blood came out of the hole and he fell over on his back, lying there, eyes open, stone-cold dead. I don't think he would have known what hit him. Then they all rose out of the undergrowth. I thought they were going to shoot me as well, but after some debate their commanding officer decided to take me prisoner. I knew immediately that he was going to interrogate me.'

The Colonel looked down at the floor and sighed. There was a break in his voice as he continued.

'I was taken to a rundown château that had been commandeered by the Germans. There I was in a boiler suit, feeling sick and shaky, waiting in an ornate room with family portraits round the walls and the shutters closed. A crystal chandelier cast a dim light over the long table.

'I felt as if I were waiting in the wide panelled room for ever, sitting at the table on one of the eight grey canvas chairs that looked incredibly dingy and out of place. There was no other furniture and I wondered if the Germans had taken it away, or whether the building had been empty for years.

'The portraits, all of idealised elderly men and women, looked disapproving. Then I noticed that one of them, a very old lady with cold eyes, had been attacked with a knife, the canvas gouged through at her left shoulder. I wondered why she had been singled out. Did she look arrogant? Or critical? Had one of the Germans decided to teach her a lesson?

'The time crept on and I kept looking down at my wristwatch. So far I'd been waiting for forty-five minutes. Was this some kind of psychological game? There had been no sign of any guards as I had been driven up the weed-covered driveway. Maybe I could just walk out. I got up stiffly and tried the door, only to find that it was locked. Then I tried one of the shutters, but they were nailed up.

'So there was no way out.

'The dim light from the chandelier flickered as if the bulbs were coming to the end of their life. I struggled with the shutters again, but they refused to budge.

'I was still struggling when I heard the door open and turned to see a middle-aged man in the doorway, dressed in the uniform of a German officer, tall, with a beaky face and a hesitant smile.

'"I'm so sorry to have kept you waiting. I speak good English so perhaps that will make what we have to discuss a little easier."

'He walked over and sat down at the head of the table, gesturing me to join him.

'There was a knock on the door and a German soldier came in with a tray of coffee and biscuits. The silver tray gleamed and the coffee service was delicate, coloured a deep blue.

'"Please join me."

'I went and sat down next to him.

'"Coffee?"

'"No thanks."

'"I would. We might be together for some time. The coffee's very good and I love the china."

'I shrugged. Trying to be assertive, I poured myself a cup of strong black coffee.

'"Cream? Biscuit?"

'"No, thanks."

'"I am Colonel Gunter Mann. And you…"

'"Ernest Springfield, Lieutenant. What do you intend to do with me?" I demanded.

'"That depends on how co-operative you are."

'"About what?"

'"French families."

'"What about them?"

'Gunter Mann paused and took an appreciative sip

of his coffee. "At the moment there is an evacuation of British troops at Dunkirk. An attempted evacuation."

"'Is there?'"

"'I'm sure you know that, Lieutenant. The French have surrendered, but there have been pockets of resistance in the surrounding countryside and we are undertaking a mopping-up operation." Gunter Mann smiled, as if we had a mutual understanding. "Some French families have been offering shelter to British soldiers."

'I said nothing, guessing what was coming next and wondering how soon the conversation, at present so civilised, would become much more threatening.

"'Quite a large number of French families have been harbouring the enemy."

'Still I said nothing.

"'So, I would appreciate knowing who they are."

"'I'm afraid I can't help you." I made eye contact with him and noticed he seemed slightly amused.

"'What a shame. But I find that hard to accept."

"'Why?'"

"'Because you and your companion were staying with a French family yourselves. We were told that a British soldier, or soldiers, were staying with the Dupois family."

"'We had ordered them to give us shelter. If they didn't comply I told Henri Dupois his family would be shot." I was sure my reply sounded weak, that my lies were obvious.

'Mann raised his eyebrows. "And now they have been."

'For a moment I wondered if he was lying, but something in his eyes told me he was not.

'"Do you think there are other French families who have been threatened in the same way?"

'"I've no idea."

'"I'm suggesting to you, Lieutenant, that you didn't use any threats. I'm suggesting that you arranged for the remainder of the men in your platoon to be sheltered by the French and that they were quite willing to do so."

'"Rubbish!"

'"Where are they then? We know you commanded a platoon." He was still extremely courteous, half-smiling, and I didn't see any point in denying my men's existence.

'"No doubt at the beaches by now, waiting for a boat. I decided it would be better for us all to go our separate ways."

'"Some of your men were wounded."

'"The French surrender left us completely exposed."

'"As you say. And as a good officer, no doubt you felt they should rest and have medical attention before trying to reach Dunkirk."

'"On the contrary. I wanted to make sure that they evacuated the area as quickly as possible."

'"Then why were you and your sergeant enjoying the comfort of a French home?"

'I knew that my answers were getting weaker, but we were both keeping up the pretence at least of holding a civilised conversation and I tried again. "We were only there one night. We were exhausted and wanted to get some sleep."

'"So you held a family at gunpoint?"

'"They were certainly very afraid."

'"How did you sleep?"

'"We each got a few hours."

'"And you took the risk of having your throat cut while you slept?"

'"Naturally one of us was awake."

'"Naturally. But my information is that you had been in the house for several days."

'"Your informants are wrong."

'"Obviously we can do a house-to-house search of all the villages in the surrounding area to find the rest of your platoon. But this would be a long and arduous process as I'm sure you can imagine."

'"I can see that."

'"We would like to take a short cut."

'"I'm afraid I can't help you."

'"Lieutenant, I'm sure you have a list of addresses where your men are staying. You were in charge and you would have intended to wait until they were rested and then move on again together."

'"I told you before, I thought we'd all do better on our own. I'm sure they've now left the area. Private Bruce and I were on our way when we were apprehended."

'"A careless mistake," said Gunter Mann.

'"Very." I would allow him that.

'There was a long silence. Then Mann asked, "More coffee?"

'"No, thank you."

'I now detected a change in his attitude, although it was very subtle. "Lieutenant, I need to know where your men are staying." There was no edge to his voice, but somehow there was a different look in his eyes.

'Once again I tried to convince him. "Look. I'm trying to make this very clear. We were all making for the beaches. We didn't have time to form a plan or find accommodation. What was left of the platoon—"

'"How many in the platoon?"

'"At the last count we had fourteen survivors," I lied, hoping Mann didn't know how many men I really had.

'"And when was this last count?"

"'A few days ago – when we were all together."

"'Then you split up?'"

"'I thought that would give us a better chance of success," I repeated.

"'You say some of your platoon were wounded."

"'You said so. But yes, some were."

"'How many?'"

"'Six."

"'They were walking wounded, I understand. But no doubt they'd have been better for a rest."

"'I didn't see any chance of that. As I've already told you, it seemed imperative to press on – to make the beaches as fast as possible." I had no idea whether I was gaining ground or not. I suspected I wasn't.

"'So why did we find two of your men at a house in Goncous? That's less than two kilometres south of here." He stirred his coffee thoughtfully, looking down at the cup.

"'I've no idea. They probably did what we did – threatened the household to snatch a night's sleep."

"'I have another way of looking at that."

"'You do?'"

"'One of your men broke down under questioning. He told us that the French Resistance had helped to give accommodation to wounded British soldiers – as well as those who were simply suffering from exhaustion. The idea was to let them rest up so they would stand a better chance of making the beaches. But we also have other concerns."

"'What are they?" I asked warily, feeling a sudden despair. I was sure now that he knew most of the facts already.

"'That these soldiers traded arms and ammunition for their period of respite."

"'That would be impossible. They didn't have any."

"'They didn't have any when we caught up with them, and that made us suspicious. Perhaps the French were desperate for arms and ammunition and gave shelter to the British in return. I wonder why? Did they have a plan? Was that it, Lieutenant?"

'I didn't reply and the Colonel began to show the first signs of irritation.

"'I need an answer, Lieutenant. And if you can't give it to me I'll get the answer I need from these French families. So you're going to tell me, *give me* a list of the exact locations of these families who gave shelter to your men."

"'There *is* no list."

"'I want the names and addresses. I want them *now*!"

"'I don't know them."

"'I believe you do." Mann stood up, his chair scraping the oak floor. "So I'm going to hand you over to my colleague."

'"Isn't that very traditional?" I felt hollow inside. I'd been afraid before – so many times – but this was the worst.

'"Traditional?"

'"The soft touch. Then the hard touch. The very roots of the Inquisition."

'"It's an old formula. But I have to tell you, Lieutenant, the old formula always works."

'When he had gone, I was subjected to another period of waiting. The passage of time seemed endless, but when I checked my watch I was amazed to see that only half an hour had passed. The chandelier was now clinking and tinkling in the draught from the half-open door, and that was a torture all of its own.'

'But if the door was half-open, couldn't you have made a run for it?' asked Patrick.

The Colonel sighed. 'There was a guard outside.' He paused and then continued. 'The door was roughly pushed open and a small man with spectacles stood on the threshold. He was carrying a large pail and was accompanied by two other men who held a couple of jugs. They were all in Gestapo uniform.

'I felt I was going to be violently sick even before they started.

'They didn't speak as they moved the bucket into the centre of the floor. The two junior officers stood on either side of it.

'The small man with the glasses sat down where Gunter Mann had been sitting and I rose quickly to my feet, holding on to the chair back.

'"I've already told your colleague I have no information. I should like to go now. The Geneva Convention stipulates—"

'"I don't think there's anywhere for you to go to, Lieutenant."

'I stared at him in silence.

'"The names."

'"I don't have any names."

'He nodded at the two men by the bucket who walked towards me, gently detached my hands from their grip on the back of the chair and pulled me over to the bucket. I didn't struggle.

'"Kneel."

'I did as I was told. The bucket was half full of water and I knew what they were going to do.

'"The names, Lieutenant."

'"I don't have any names."

'A soldier grabbed the back of my neck and forced my head into the bucket and held it there. I struggled desperately, but he was immensely strong and he kept me down for a long time. When I began to choke and swallow water he pulled me out by the hair and I collapsed on the floor, throwing up. I had never been so afraid; there wasn't even a merciful feeling of numbness.

'"The names."

'"I don't have them," I gasped.

'One of the soldiers carefully filled the bucket again to the same prescribed level.

'Then the other soldier held me down. He was much rougher and kept my head below the surface until I was choking so hard that I thought I was going to drown, water flooding into my nose and ears and mouth.

'After what seemed an eternity, my head was yanked out of the bucket again.

'"The names," the small man whispered. "I'd rather we didn't have to continue. Give me the names."

'"I don't have them – I swear to God. There's no list, no names, no addresses." I choked out the words as I retched up gobs of phlegm.

'They put my head in the bucket again and this time held me there for much longer until, amongst the choking and swallowing and flailing and panic, I felt the impossible tightening of my chest.

'They yanked me out at the last moment.

'I lay on my front, vomiting, the pain in my chest so great that I could only breathe in little gasps.

'"The names," said the small man relentlessly. "Give me the names."'

'But you didn't give them the names,' said Patrick, gazing at the Colonel who was sitting on the edge of the ragged old chair, his head in his hands, breathing in little gasps, his thin shoulders heaving. 'You didn't give them the names, did you?'

Still the Colonel didn't look up and Patrick began to sweat. Suddenly his refusal to give the Gestapo the names seemed the most important thing in the world.

'Tell me you didn't give them the names.'

Slowly the Colonel looked up at Patrick like a helpless wounded animal. 'I gave them the names.'

There was a terrible silence.

'I also gave them the addresses and the details of which men were at which houses. I gave them the names of the families who were hiding them. I gave them everything they wanted, including the details about the plan to ambush the train.'

The silence deepened.

'Anything to prevent them putting my head in the bucket again.'

An even longer silence.

'For God's sake, say something,' said the Colonel.

'Thousands of people break under torture.' Patrick's voice was flat.

'Do you know,' continued the Colonel very quietly, 'I've never dared to put my head under water again. Not in the pool, not in the sea, not in the lake, not anywhere.'

'What happened?' asked Patrick.

'What the hell do you mean, what happened!' He was furious now.

'To the families.'

'Every single one of them, including the children and old people, were executed.'

'And the soldiers?'

'Declared missing. I know they were shot. I've lived with the fear that one or two may have survived and would hunt me down. That's why I moved out here.'

Patrick said nothing.

'Say something, for Christ's sake.'

'Most people break down under torture,' repeated Patrick mechanically. Then he added, 'I wasn't even being tortured when I grassed Jim up.'

'But your mother was being threatened.'

'I still grassed on him.'

The tears suddenly flooded down the Colonel's withered cheeks. 'I didn't even have your excuse. I've lived with my cowardice ever since. No one knows the truth – except you. I fooled them all – even Sandra.' The Colonel sank back into his chair. Then he reached out automatically for the whisky and discovered the bottle was empty. He threw it at the photograph of Tom. Both smashed at the same time.

Glass flew everywhere and instinctively Patrick covered his face. 'I need you to protect me,' he half-whispered.

'How can I protect anyone? You lost the damn gun. Anyway, I'm no use to you. I'm a coward. And even worse, I pursued my army career and was considered a very distinguished soldier,' said the Colonel bitterly. 'I lived the lie and did pretty well out of it, didn't I?'

This time Patrick didn't even offer a polite protest, knowing that nothing he could say would wipe out the Colonel's guilt. He wondered what would have happened if the old man had used his school visit to tell this terrible, sad story. The lads would have laughed. The girls might have understood.

The lads would have *had* to laugh. They would have watched each other, making sure they were all laughing. But the girls would have made up their own minds.

Patrick knew he hadn't made up his. Not yet, anyway. He began to think of Tom and how the Colonel had suffered such grief.

There was a deep silence between them, which was interrupted by a single knock on the trapdoor. Then the knock came again.

FOURTEEN

'How did they find us?' whispered the Colonel.

'Maybe they were hiding,' said Patrick. 'Maybe they watched us come over from the lake.' His head was aching again. Badly now. Patrick felt hot and cold in turns. Had his wound brought on a fever?

'They waited a hell of a long time.'

'They're good at waiting.'

Again the knock.

'Or it was a process of elimination.' The Colonel was still worrying at the problem. What was the point? Patrick wondered. All that mattered was that Cal had finally come. Curiously, Patrick almost felt a sense of relief. He was calm, ready, almost eager to take his punishment. Time was no longer on hold.

Suddenly the trapdoor was pulled open and the steely light of dawn filtered into the crypt.

'Careful!' hissed Cal. 'The old bastard's got a gun.'

'The old bastard hasn't,' said the Colonel before Patrick could stop him.

Then he saw the barrel of a revolver and Patrick realised what had taken them so long. They'd gone to get their own weapons so they could play the Colonel at his own game. Cal and his family would definitely ignore decommissioning, Patrick thought. But so, apparently, had Jim.

'Walk up the steps,' said Cal triumphantly. 'Walk up with your hands raised – and leave your shotgun down there.'

'I haven't got it any longer.'

'Where is it?' rasped Cal.

'In the lake.'

'That was careless.'

There was muted laughter, interrupted by Connor's awful giggle.

'I'll go first,' said the Colonel. He seemed full of authority. Patrick was amazed. A few minutes ago he had collapsed in drunken self-pity. Now he seemed very much in charge.

'They don't want you,' said Patrick. 'They only want me.'

'We want the two of you. Drunk or sober.' Cal's voice was full of contempt.

The Colonel lurched towards the ladder and climbed unsteadily.

Patrick followed and Cal laughed. 'The old man smells like a distillery.'

There were only four of them. Cal, Seamus, Connor and Dermot. Cal had a gun and so did Seamus. Had the others taken Felix to hospital? wondered Patrick.

'Are you going to use those guns on me?' he asked.

'We haven't decided yet,' said Cal.

'Thanks a bunch.'

'Now listen to me.' The Colonel still seemed full of authority. 'You can't take the law into your own hands.'

'You did,' said Cal, and Patrick had never felt such hatred. Looking at their grim faces he was sure they were going to kill him. Then he caught Dermot's eye.

'I'm sorry about your dad,' Patrick tried.

'Shut your mouth – for once.' Dermot was white with rage. 'I don't want to hear your voice, understand?'

The certainty of death made Patrick numb and he thought of Mum and Declan. Were they already dead? Had Cal already killed them? Were his precious loved ones still lying in the house, or had they already been taken to the mortuary?

The Colonel turned to Patrick. 'I've built up a lot of respect for this young man tonight.'

'And I've built up a lot of respect for the Colonel,' said Patrick, surprising himself.

'OK,' continued the Colonel. 'We've both admitted that we've cheated. How about you? How many times have you cheated?'

Cal simply laughed. 'What a load of crap.' He moved nearer to the Colonel, the gun pointing at his chest. 'You're an old piss-pot – that's all you are.'

The plaster on Cal's nose made him look slightly ridiculous, but Patrick also knew that he'd never seen him look so grim.

'Give me the gun,' said the Colonel and then glanced at Seamus. 'And yours.'

The Colonel moved confidently towards Cal, hand outstretched, and to his surprise Patrick saw that, for once, Cal was hesitating, almost dithering, and Seamus had his gun aimed at the floor rather than at the Colonel.

'Give me the guns,' he repeated.

'To hell with you,' said Cal, and shot the Colonel at point-blank range.

Patrick watched the Colonel stagger back, blood welling from his chest, flooding out of the hole in his dressing gown. He clutched at the entry wound, hit the wall and then gradually slid to the ground.

Patrick couldn't believe what had happened. After all they had been through, the Colonel had been wiped out. Just like that. Patrick felt he was breaking up, that the world was ending.

Cal said nothing, staring down at the Colonel curiously. Was this the first man he'd shot? wondered Patrick.

'Let's be going,' said Seamus, backing away. But Dermot was gazing down as curiously as Cal.

Connor looked cowed, unable to really take in what had happened or make a decision about what should happen next. His giggle seemed to have left him.

For some reason he couldn't explain, Patrick suddenly remembered his mobile and dragged it out of his pocket. He wanted to call an ambulance or the police, or even his mum and Declan, if they were still alive. But Cal brought the gun down on his wrist, the flooding pain making Patrick drop the phone on the floor.

Cal stomped on the mobile until it was crushed. Just like the Colonel had crushed the photograph frame.

'You've got to get help for him,' pleaded Patrick.

'Not until you've had one hell of a beating,' said Cal.

'Get on and beat me then.' Patrick was watching the Colonel twitching. 'You've got to get help.'

'Come on, Cal. We can phone from the call box down the road.' Dermot was suddenly anxious to get going.

'Hasn't anyone else got a mobile?' Patrick felt curiously in charge, as if not only the Colonel's leadership had slipped away but Cal's as well.

Connor, Seamus and Cal's eyes were on the Colonel, whose breathing was now painfully shallow.

'For God's sake,' began Dermot from the doorway.

His voice was shrill. 'We'll be on a murder charge if he dies. Call an ambulance, Cal.'

'And get caught?' Cal looked at Patrick, almost as if he was needing his advice.

'Who's got a mobile?'

They all shook their heads.

'Cal?'

'I haven't got it with me, so help me God.' Was Cal beginning to sound panicky? 'What about the phone in the house?'

'It doesn't work.'

'You cut the cable,' Dermot reminded Cal. 'We'll have to get down the road bloody fast.'

It was as if they were all united, of one mind, old friends who had to avoid being caught.

Cal put the gun away in his pocket and began to run.

So did the others.

Patrick yelled over his shoulder, 'I'll be back. I'll be back with some help. You've got to keep going until then.'

As he glanced back at the Colonel, Patrick saw that his eyes were closed.

FIFTEEN

They sprinted through the wilderness of long grass to the wall that surrounded the grounds and then helped each other over, Cal bunking them up, and then running and grabbing at the top of the wall himself, relying on his strength to get over.

Now, with Cal in the lead, they began to run through the dense wood until Patrick was sure – absolutely sure – they were lost.

He came to a halt. 'We're going the wrong way.'

'How do you know that?' demanded Dermot, while Connor bowed his head and put his hands on his knees. So did Cal.

'We have to keep going south,' said Patrick urgently.

'Are you lying?' asked Cal, looking up ominously.

'He can't die on us. We've *got* to get help.' It was as if Patrick were a member of the gang and not their victim any longer. 'We speak the same language.'

'What do you mean by that?' asked Seamus.

'It's a secret language.' He suddenly remembered an old documentary he'd seen on TV of two opposing armies crossing no-man's-land and embracing each other on Christmas Day.

Patrick began to run through the undergrowth.

'What secrets were you talking?' yelled Cal.

'We got together,' Patrick gasped. 'We lied and then told the truth. That doesn't happen much.'

They were all stumbling through the undergrowth, tearing their hands on brambles, gasping in the humid dawn.

'You're leading us in circles,' yelled Cal.

Yes, I am leading you, thought Patrick. I'm heading for the telephone box. But already another voice inside was telling him over and over again that the Colonel was dead. He couldn't survive a bullet in the chest. How could anyone – let alone an old man?

Still he ran on.

'There's the road,' Patrick shouted, but Cal paused.

'Let's leave him to die there.'

They had all come to a halt now, standing in a circle round Patrick.

'Go back there,' said Cal, suddenly breaking the silence.

'Wait a minute,' began Dermot.

'No,' said Cal. He spoke very slowly, as if he were trying to reason things out, as if he wanted everyone to understand. 'Get back over the wall,' he said.

'What?' Patrick stared at him uncomprehendingly.

'I said, get back over that bloody wall. Go and bury your Colonel.'

'But Patrick has to have a beating,' said Dermot.

'He's had a beating,' said Cal. He punched Patrick hard on the shoulder and Patrick reeled back.

The circle parted.

'You're a casualty of war,' said Cal. He hit Patrick again. 'Go and bury your old man.'

Cal turned to the gang and Patrick wondered if they would obey him. Could there be a mutiny?

'Come on then,' said Cal. 'Let's get going.' He looked down at his torch and then gave it to Patrick.

Patrick watched Cal begin to run. The others hesitated. Then they began to run too. Soon they had disappeared into the darkness.

As Patrick scrambled back over the wall he thought, casualties of war. That's what we are. All of us, even Cal.

He ran back through the long grass to the summer house and swung around the torch that Cal had given him, picking up the slumped body of the Colonel.

Patrick began to pray. 'Holy Mother of Jesus, let him be alive. Holy Mother of Jesus – he's got to live, do you hear? Do you hear me, God?'

But the Colonel's eyes were open now, staring ahead, and Patrick knew he was dead. Nevertheless he grabbed his wrist and tried to find a pulse. There wasn't one.

'I'll breathe the air back into your lungs, you miserable old bastard,' yelled Patrick at the dead Colonel.

He pulled at the Colonel's stick-like legs until he was flat on the floor of the summer house. He'd learnt to do the kiss of life years ago when he was in the Cubs, but he had largely forgotten the process. In spite of this he tried, putting his mouth to the Colonel's and blowing as hard as he could. But nothing happened, and eventually after five minutes or so, Patrick gave up trying. He knew the Colonel was dead and nothing he could do was going to make any difference.

Patrick stood helplessly beside the body, wondering what to do. Then suddenly he knew. The Colonel should go to the place he had created for Sandra and rest beside her.

Leaving the summer house, Patrick searched in the undergrowth, looking for the two implements that he was sure he would find.

Then the early morning light flickered on the wheelbarrow and a spade. Had they been used for Sandra's burial? Undignified, but practical? Patrick took at least five minutes dragging the barrow out of the bushes and another few minutes extracting the spade.

While he was sweating away Patrick wondered if he'd be done for murder. Well, he hadn't shot the old man, had he? But no one was going to know that, and all the witnesses would say it was him, not Cal. And now, here he was about to illicitly bury the body without an inquest or post-mortem or any of the niceties.

But it felt right.

Dumping the wheelbarrow outside the summer house, Patrick went back inside and checked the Colonel yet again. He was dead all right. The wound in his chest had stopped bleeding, the blood congealing.

'Come on, you,' he said aloud, and bent down, gathering the old man up in his arms. He was as light as a feather, like a dead bird with tiny bones, or maybe more like one of Declan's crane flies, light and spindly, weighing nothing at all.

Gently Patrick carried the Colonel outside and put him in the wheelbarrow.

'Sorry about this,' he said.

Then Patrick added the spade, lifted the handles of the wheelbarrow and shoved the torch in the Colonel's dressing-gown pocket. He began to wheel the body, bumping over the long grass of the lawn on his way down to the lake.

When he arrived at the bank, Patrick pulled the Colonel's body out of the wheelbarrow and walked slowly over to the jetty and the dinghy that the

Colonel had secured. He gently dumped the old bones into the boat, jumped in himself and cast off. The body lay awkwardly over the seat so he couldn't use the rowlocks properly and had to propel the dinghy erratically towards the island.

As he moved slowly over the dark water, Patrick looked down into the Colonel's staring eyes and whispered, 'You could be King Arthur. And I'm one of your knights, rowing you to the burial grounds. To – where was it? Avalon?'

Then the dinghy bumped against the foreshore of the island. Pulling it up the muddy bank, Patrick grabbed the spade, leaving the Colonel on his back, staring up at the fading moon.

Patrick knew the digging was going to be the toughest part of the deal, but he had not expected the ground to be so hard. He had chosen a spot beside the other grave and it took Patrick at least an hour's digging before he was satisfied that he was making progress.

Then, having taken off his shirt, he dug for another hour after that. The sweat ran cold over his chest and down his back as he worked. But eventually Patrick was satisfied that he had dug deep enough.

Staggering, exhausted and gasping for breath, he returned to the dinghy and picked up the Colonel's body.

He carried him to the grave, lightly kissing the old man's forehead and then crouching down so that he could gently lower the Colonel into his resting place.

Patrick stared down at him for a moment.

He could smell whisky.

Standing up, and with his arm muscles screaming, he began to spade the earth back on to the Colonel.

It took a long time.

He'd given up looking at his watch.

At last he straightened up. Walking stiffly to the muddy shoreline, he threw the spade as far as he could into the lake.

Returning to the mound, Patrick knelt down and said the Hail Mary.

Then he got up and pushed the dinghy back into the water. Slowly he began to row back across the lake.

Patrick didn't look back.

Then he wondered about the Colonel's cat. He'd have to make sure the door was open.

Orchard Black Apples

☐ **The Drop**	*Anthomy Masters*	1 84362 196 7
☐ **Little Soldier**	*Bernard Ashley*	1 86039 879 0
☐ **Revenge House**	*Bernard Ashley*	1 84121 814 6
☐ **Tiger Without Teeth**	*Bernard Ashley*	1 84362 204 1
☐ **Going Straight**	*Michael Coleman*	1 84362 299 8
☐ **Tag**	*Michael Coleman*	1 84362 182 7
☐ **Weirdo's War**	*Michael Coleman*	1 84362 183 5
☐ **Horowitz Horror**	*Anthony Horowitz*	1 84121 455 8
☐ **More Horowitz Horror**	*Anthony Horowitz*	1 84121 607 0
☐ **The Mighty Crashman**	*Jerry Spinelli*	1 84121 222 9
☐ **Stargirl**	*Jerry Spinelli*	1 84121 926 6
☐ **Get a Life**	*Jean Ure*	1 84121 831 6

All priced at £4.99

Orchard Black Apples are available from all good bookshops,
or can be ordered direct from the publisher:
Orchard Books, PO BOX 29, Douglas IM99 1BQ
Credit card orders: please telephone 01624 836000 or fax 01624 837033
or visit our Internet site: www.wattspub.co.uk
or e-mail: bookshop@enterprise.net for details.

To order please quote title, author and ISBN
and your full name and address.
Cheques and postal orders should be made payable to 'Bookpost plc.'
Postage and packing is FREE within the UK
(overseas customers should add £1.00 per book).
Prices and availability are subject to change.